Praise for *T*

"Visi[onary]
*Steven M[o...] former*
*Doctor Who* snowrunner

"A psychedelic thriller that reinvents the form [...] a mind bending story of possibility."
*Tenacity Plys*, author of
*Family Curse: Field Notebooks* (1880-2020)

———

Praise for Jules Pelarski

"i feel like i just lost my mind and then u gently handed it back to me"
*-lamphouse*

"I am positively reeling right now."
*-Perugno*

"Holy shit."
*-R.C. MacLachlan*

"Stark, emotionally dense, haunting, terrifying, and yet, still, just a bit hopeful. Perfect."
*-AfroGeekGoddess*

# TEMPUS
# *FUGIT*

## VOL I: THE ENGAGEMENT RING

*jules pelarski*

*For my friend Steve*
*who was really there.*

All of this happened, more or less.

— KURT VONNEGUT

# PROLOGUE

Dear Reader,
 This story is a true story and it is a rather long story not to mention an unbelievable story which is why I have begun to write it down.

It was told for the first time under a bridge in San Francisco, to a group of raggedy strangers wrapped in blankets. We had a good dumpster fire going. I had gone full Kanye, evaded the authorities, and found companionship with the other vagrants. They listened. Really listened, too, not the blank-eyed kind, and while they, like my family and friends, were concerned, they reacted with calm, unaffected reassurance rather than panic-inducing worry or fear.

To wit, I wasn't alone, not once, even at the very end. More and more of us are coming together under the bridge and we are there for each other, and that is why there isn't going to be an apocalypse.

That's the short version.

But there was a time I did not know this. You, in fact,

may still not know it. You, like me, may worry about the state of this or that and how it's all going to happen. Well, my friend, I have good news: I'm a time traveler from 2035, carrying with me a contraband fragment of future.

Though documents exist that predate the October incident (see: The Venus Papers), this account concerns itself only with the Ring Box Paradox and all incidents thereafter. Some details have been changed to protect continuity (but you're clever, you'll figure it out).

Maybe you won't believe me. Hey, people won't. I'm used to it. But if you do? Meet me under the bridge in San Francisco. There's a story I'm telling.


Yours truly,
    The One Eyed Jack

# 1

## THE BEGINNING

It was the end of the world and there was nothing you could do about it. It said so on billboards, it blared from television sets, it whispered out of the little box of light you always carried with you: strikes, fires, floods. It passed by as a casual joke, a scream on the street, a lyric in a love song. Those, those were the days.

You were there.

You worked nights at a gas station Qwik Mart owned by a trio of men named Patel. Quiet life far from the city. At sunrise you'd longboard home to the RV you shared with your best friend Berlin, stationed in an abandoned trailer park close enough to the flooded shore you could always hear the ocean. It calmed you, the consistency. The certainty could swallow you up and wash this all away.

It was a day like that when it all began. You: powerless, ordinary, nothing. The sky: pre-sun red. The ocean: wailing, ever present. Time: passing by.

There was a river of grief inside you, too, something you did not look at and could not name. You were growing up and going nowhere. The strings that tied you to home were snapping. Love had carved its hole in you and the ache to fill it would not be satisfied.

But you were getting ahead of yourself. Time and time again: running, reaching out, falling short. Trapped in a whirlpool of fantasy and memory that bled together like watercolor dawn.

Berlin was trouble. You liked this about him. A dreamer, a drummer, and a drug dealer, Berlin had turned his talents to synthesizers somewhere around the turn of the decade. The dark night clubs where Berlin performed were the perfect place to peddle his wares, and his proclivity for similarly synthesized hallucinogens produced "some of the most unique beats of our generation," according to an online zine named "FUCK PUNK" that hardly mattered.

Berlin didn't mind. Berlin considered acknowledgement from any authority a kind of insult. He purposefully snuck dissonant chords into his compositions, protests against form and function. He was a sociology major before he dropped out of the liberal arts college you attended together—he failed a mandatory math class and lost his financial aid. But even this Berlin did with a high chin: he bought the RV, parked it by the beach, and hosted his first party the very night he was expelled.

Yes, you were there. It was a good life. The world was burning, and there was nothing you could do.

There it was again: the ache you could not ignore. The fear and uncertainty, the future a lion crouched at the mouth of a cave. That morning, you had asked the girl you loved to marry you. She said 'no.'

The rings belonged to your great grandmother. Diamonds. Modest, but valuable enough to be the most expensive item you'd ever owned. You'd taken the blue velvet box from your mother's dresser the night you ran off with Berlin, claiming your inheritance. You didn't know when you'd be back again. You never knew when you'd find it: love.

You sat across from Violet Hunter in the Red Arrow Diner, a tiny railcar place in the center of town, open all hours. It was raining. The raindrops made fractals on the windows as they made impact, then hurried away.

Violet was a senior, now. Bound for Law School. You almost felt guilty: gas station layabout courts promising candidate for valedictorian. Her dad, an LA executive at Vestal Entertainment, didn't like it either — you had visited her home that summer and he'd done everything in his power to make you feel unwelcome. It made sense, of course: you were a corrupting influence. You stood in the way of Violet's success. But here she was, dating you anyway. It was that rebellious streak that drew you to her in the first place: the revolutionary who could go toe to toe with Berlin when the situation demanded, who snuck away from snobby student government parties to dance to arrhythmic beats in a shady club on the outskirts of town. She wore a nose ring in her right nostril that only you knew was fake. And she was an optimist.

But lately, since arriving back on campus, things had felt different. It was as though her dad had sat her down, given her a good talking to, and made a genuine impression. You could feel her weighing the scales whenever you were together, wondering if you were right, getting ready to pull away. Now was the moment, you thought, to show her what you wanted. To commit.

You turned away from the memory.

TO GO TO WORK, *continue reading on the next page.*

# 2
———

Work as cashier at a Qwik Mart gave you plenty of time to fret: dead space, small talk, and lots of fluorescent light. The shifts inched by infinite, but when you left, they were compressed into a single polaroid frame and burned away by a joint. And the people that passed by: vagrants, construction workers, even the President of Royal Oaks college, in sweatpants, not knowing you recognized him. Not knowing that this was what his education got you: an RV and a girl who said 'no.' *Here I am at the end of the world, peddling lottery.* At the end of the night, you'd sweep up the losing tickets that'd been littered by the meters. *Not a winner! Not a winner! Not a winner!*

Gas prices went up.

Time went by.

There was a new drug Berlin wanted. Something designer, something real underground. "I'm not even sure it's real," he told you, his eyes alight with the promise of it. "But I'm sticking my feelers out."

"What could possibly be more enticing than valentine?" you asked (a smokable cannabis aphrodisiac, dyed pink).

"*This,*" said Berlin, giving you nothing. He turned his attention back to his laptop screen.

You started dreaming about storms. You were familiar with the drowned outskirts from your travels, the famous newsreel of the sunken city, but now you were being battered about in a little rowboat, civilization coming down around you, or else you were in the RV as it was swept away by the outraged ocean, all that water seeping in. It'd pitch to one side and you'd roll off the sofa bed, tossed into a disoriented moment where you thought you'd gotten wet. And at work, after coming back from a spliff break, your eyes would play tricks on you as they saw and un-saw a subtle leak in the ceiling by the door.

Perhaps you think such a thing would alarm you. But this is the future, and these are but drugs and dreams.

"I found a connect," Berlin said much later. "He's not happy I found him. But I'm finished the hard part."

"Should I worry about people coming after us?"

"Shut up," said Berlin. "He has no idea where we live."

Your stomach clenched.

The worst trouble Berlin ever got in was about three months back. It was your first night back at the Royal Oaks and he was tripping balls. You weren't there when it began, but at the end, he was taken away kicking and screaming by no less than four firefighters that he swore at until they sedated him. He was held up North in Clearview Hospital for two weeks.

You visited him there.

"The doctor here is a Russian spy," he'd said. He was in clothes from the hospital lost and found: too-short sweatpants with tight cuffs and a boxy, flamboyant button-up with a pattern from a bowling alley floor. He kept his arms crossed and his eyes on your Achilles' heel, scowling. "They're after you, too."

The nurses had instructed you how to act. "Okay."

"'Okay?' That's it?"

"I'm just here to see you."

Berlin laughed, a bitter chuckle.

"I'm sorry," you said.

Berlin met your eye. "They won't let me out of here."

"I know."

"They're keeping people trapped in here. There's a lady in here, they're saying she's paranoid. But it's not paranoia. It's *completely fucking legit,* and I'd be next on the chopping block, but I've got the smarts to keep my mouth shut."

You took his advice: kept your mouth shut.

He nodded, rolled his eyes, and looked askance. Now back to you, gaze black serious. "You gotta get me outta here."

You didn't know what to say. "You were sectioned."

"I didn't sign the damn thing. I was *threatened.* Thought I'd get a lawyer. But they wouldn't let me do jack shit til I signed my rights away."

"Yeah, I guess that's how they do it."

"And they're drugging me." Berlin smirked. "But it'll take a lot more than that."

"Lin..."

"What?" Wild eyes.

He was clearly high, paranoid, *something*. He'd be safe here.

To HELP BERLIN HEAL, *continue reading on the next page*.

*To enable Berlin's delusion, go to page* 13

## 3

The hospital awed you in a terrible, frigid way, all objective and white. What a horrible place to be trapped, you thought. But needs must.

"Berlin, what do you expect me to do, sneak you out under a trenchcoat? Seduce a security guard? Get thrown in here myself? You can't ask me to do this."

Berlin crossed his arms across his chest and grumbled something about "the wheel of the fucking establishment."

"Berlin..." you had to ask. "What was it you *took?*"

Berlin shook his head. "Nothing. Don't remember."

"That doesn't sound like you. See? I'm worried. That's all."

He wasn't looking at you anymore. Back to your Achilles heel. "I don't want a visitor anymore."

"Ok," you replied, holding your hands up in entreaty. "Ok. I'll go."

Under his breath: "Good."

You left. The nurses had said not to take any of it

personally. He was confused. Distressed. Disturbed, but healing.

On your way out, you stopped by a large wall that displayed portraits of all the doctors working at the hospital. You searched for Berlin's doctor, a man named Kozlov. He was an unsmiling grey-haired man with facial hair. Cold, dead eyes. He could have been anyone.

You picked Berlin up when he was released and took him to his favorite drive thru. He didn't talk about it.

"Thank God I'm out of there," he said, and that was all.

To TAKE BERLIN HOME, *turn to page* 15

# 4

---

F uck it. This was the place where it all began. Who are you to say what's wrong and right, true and false, sane or crazy? Why not trust your friend over this institution? There was even a feeling of premonition tapping on your shoulder, telling you here was where you'd make it right, here was the place you'd hold onto. The hospital: sterile, white, and humming. The future: a wide, imagined plane.

"You're right. We need to get you out of here. Do you have a plan?"

"We'll figure it out." Berlin said. He was on one of those grey government-issue chairs, and now he was winding around, warping the metal and plastic. "There's something I need to tell you..."

"What?"

"It's complicated. I don't want you to think I'm crazy."

"I don't think you're crazy."

"You don't know what I'm about to say."

You paused, waited politely.

"I... when I was tripping, I started... remembering things. No, hear me out, I mean... things that... haven't happened. Or... or haven't happened *yet*." He untwisted his chair but wouldn't meet your eye, instead studying the patterns on the floor. You studied them with him. "I swear. Something's going on. I'm not crazy."

"I don't think you're crazy," you said again.

"Then why am I in here then? You've got to get me out of here. Then I can get to the bottom of it."

The nurses were issuing a five minute warning. Berlin didn't seem to notice.

"Do you know where to find the Delta Tango Hotel?"'

*If you know where to find it, turn to page* 18

*If you don't know where to find it, turn to page* 20

**5**

---

He'd been subdued after that. Slow to return to his work and his music. The meds made him sleep, heavy and dreamless. He spent hours on his laptop, turned away from you, dead-eyed staring. Your mind ran worried circles around itself trying to understand him, to fix it. To remember something you'd forgotten. Then, one day, he knew.

He didn't tell you right at first, but in hindsight, you sensed immediately a change in his aura. He'd brightened up, keen with something. The connect. Before he told you, he returned to his music, pulling his synthpad out from under the bed to indulge in compositions that were stranger than ever before: erratic, arrhythmic and out of tempo. They looped in on themselves and meandered along expressionistic alleys of scale while the same bizarre beat boop-booped around underneath them.

When he was satisfied, he stepped out of the RV to make some phone calls on his burner. A new burner, as a matter of fact. Then, he took the RV to a subway station, left you there, and didn't come back for days. When he did, he took your shoulder in hand and gently shook you awake, late at night.

"I got it," he said, voice hushed. "I fucking got it."

You can remember exactly what you'd been dreaming about: a terrible flood at the Red Arrow diner. Water was even coming in through the ceiling. President Girlfriend was nowhere to be found. You could feel the weight of the water as you pushed through it, up to your thighs. And someone was sneaking up behind you—! which must have been Berlin.

"I'm up, I'm up! Got what?"

He held up what appeared in the dark to be an unremarkable scrap of paper. "4D-LSD. Area 51. Not a scam."

"That's a scam."

"It's *legit!*" Berlin said, folding the sheet in two and tucking it into his shirt pocket. "It's... it's... How long have I been gone?"

You searched around for your phone in the dark. 3 in the morning. "I don't know," you mumbled. "A while?"

Berlin laughed.

"Berlin?"

"This is a fucking *trip,*" he said, quietly.

"Do you need to go to the hospital?"

"No. *Fuck,* no. You want me turned into a biology frog?"

Not entirely reassured, you asked, "What happened?"

Again, it took Berlin a long moment to answer. "It's a long story. And I may have hallucinated half of it. So I guess we'll just have to wait and see." It was raining.

"You're telling me that little piece of paper came out of Area 51, but I just have to 'wait and see?'"

"It's more than 'a little piece of paper,' show some respect."

"'4D-LSD.' You're serious?"

"Yeah. Wanna try?"

To ACCEPT, *turn to page 22*
    *To refuse, turn to page 24*
    *To question Berlin, turn to page 31*

## 6

––––––––

Berlin smiled. "I thought I saw it flickering in you. Welcome to the trip." He studied your face for a moment. "You with me? Can you remember things that haven't happened yet?"

It was hard to say. 'Delta Tango Hotel' meant something to you without your full understanding, and with it was a cluster of certainties that were not quite memories, but also more than dreams. It was deja vu times a dozen, time stretched out like the inevitable spiral of a slinky. You were poised again at the top of the stairwell, all anticipation. The edges of your vision shimmered like the air on a hot day.

"I went way, way out," Berlin said, "but it goes in both directions."

He looked crazy when he said it: unhinged, eyes too wide and lopsided. But the insanity of it all was what kept you here: indecisive, lingering. The echoes of your future were fading, but they left in their wake a certainty that Berlin needed your help, to trust him.

"What do you want me to do?" you asked.

"Set a fire," Berlin shrugged, eyebrows up, almost smiling. Manic, manic. "I don't know."

"You serious?"

"It's the only thing I can think of. They'd have to evacuate."

"Why don't you just wait it out?"

"It's awful," Berlin said. "I think they're erasing me."

"Erasing you? Erasing you how?"

"I don't know how, but I can feel it."

The head nurse announced to the room that visiting hours had ended.

TO SET A FIRE, *turn to page 32*

*To pick him up in a week when he's released, turn to page 15*

## 7

---

"**D**on't worry about it," Berlin said, waving it off. "You'll figure it out soon enough. I'll call you, they have pay phones." You had indeed seen the shiny black phones in their little boxes on your way in. You'd assumed they didn't work. "We'll figure it out."

He smiled like he meant it.

BUT BERLIN DIDN'T CALL.

You were riddled with increasingly disturbing dreams: wandering through hospital halls, Berlin silhouetted in the red EXIT sign glow. Elevators and locked doors. Driving the RV down narrow alleys. And water, always water washing over you at the end, washing you out where you'd wake up listening as the waves went in and out, in and out.

It was Friday. Next visiting hours weren't until Wednesday. There was no use calling, you'd tried to get through for hours when he was first sectioned. There was just no getting in.

It was a rainy season.

When you saw Berlin again, the facility was shrouded in thick, white fog. You couldn't see a thing outside the windows. Berlin was in uniform sweatsuit gray, with the hood pulled up over his head. There were no drawstrings in the hoodie, just two holes where they should have been. He didn't want to talk to you.

*TO PICK Berlin up in a week when he's released, turn to page 15*

## 8

### DELTA TANGO HOTEL

Berlin ripped off a little square for you no bigger than the nail of your pinky finger. "Just put it on your tongue and let it dissolve. It should start working right away, but it takes a few hours to really settle in."

Balancing the tab on your finger in the dim glow of Berlin's fairy lights, you saw that each perforated square of acid had printed on it a cartoon bunny with vortexes for eyes.

"And you're sure it won't turn my brain to scrambled eggs?"

"I'm standing here, aren't I?"

You dropped the tab onto your tongue. Tasted like sweet paper.

"As you fall in, it helps to anchor your trip to something, a space in time. Your perception gets... wider, and it can be overwhelming. But it's just like going to a happy place or good memory. Try not to lose your cool."

Already the tab moistened and flaked apart.

"If you can, find me. Try to help me."

"Help you?" You spoke funny with the tab still dissolving. "Help you with what?"

"With everything," he smiled. "Like you usually do."

"I don't—"

"Take these," Berlin said, folding the square of tabs in half and pressing them into your pocket. "You never know when you might need them."

The tab was gone.

*T URN to page 34 to start tripping*

## 9

# A CAUTIONARY TALE

H*ere.* At the head of everything. Stop it. Stop it now, before it all goes wrong. Your gut was black with premonition, the moment of it crystallized and sharp.

"Berlin, we shouldn't do this. We *can't* do this. It's going to end bad."

Berlin smiled. "No it isn't."

"What do you mean, 'no it isn't?'"

"It isn't. Because you're here saying that now."

"What?"

"Anything bad that happened to me is in your past. So you're here to change it into a future where things are fixed."

Even as he said this, the future went blurry, blurrier, and you knew it would soon go black. You could feel the pre-high receding, almost not-there, like a dream upon waking. The harder you focused, the further away it felt. You weren't sure of your own memory, it felt like an imagined thing.

"Listen, I feel it, too," said Berlin. "I'm seeing in seven different directions right now. But you *can't panic.* I think that's the worst thing."

And then, the walls bloomed, taunting you. It was coming back. You pressed your palms hard against your eyes til you saw dull purple fireworks. "Who the fuck do you think you are? I'm trying to be fucking serious here, we have to *stop this!*"

"What'd I just say?!"

"I am trying! To save! Our lives!"

"Ok. Ok. Listen, I don't know for sure, but that *might* be a paradox."

"It 'MIGHT'?!" The ocean outside roared with you.

"Shh, shh! Stay calm! It's hard to say it's impossible, but with the way the universe patches itself up, it's highly unlikely."

"'Stay calm?' 'Stay calm?' I've got half-imagined futures dissolving my frontal lobe, and your advice is 'stay calm?'"

The ocean, the waves. The RV seemed to rock.

"Yes! Can't you see what's happening?"

You stood and made your way to the front of the RV, but the pre-trip altered your depth perception, and you fell. You stumbled forward, catching yourself and not quite falling, but when you straightened, you were somewhere else. You were in a dark club in the city—the *Delta Variant,* one of Berlin's favorite haunts.

"Wha...?" you wondered, peering around in the dark, the throbbing music so thick it was nearly a veil. You recognized one of Berlin's beats. Pink lights spun around the club, interspersed with flashes of neon green; purple smoke lingered around guests on the dance floor as if just expelled by caterpillar.

The *Delta Variant* was a tiny, grungy lounge on the outskirts of the Royal Oaks with a broken neon sign and a bad reputation. Berlin was largely responsible for the latter, but the poor lighting, dank acoustics, and broken bar mirror didn't help. Berlin had struck up a deal with the owner a few years after he began his entrepreneurial endeavors, convincing him he had an online following from the college scene that would pay through the nose for overpriced beers and Supercokes. He was a salesman, and he made good on his promises. Even now, eight years out, he supplied a steady stream of undergrads on the hunt for the most exclusive high.

Is that what you were doing here? Was he passing out time tabs to the world, just like that?

Your memory stalled, skipping like a broken record. Something was off about where you were. What was it?

The employees of the *Variant* were all heavily tattooed and pierced, generous with liquor and stingy with smiles. They kept up with what was not fashionable and played along with all the anti-trends in artsy, niche t-shirts and vintage Tripp pants. Berlin's drugs were fashionable. It was a perfect match.

One of his songs was blaring, thwanging and thumping. It wasn't exactly danceable, but people were trying, as if even to dance were an act of defiance. The music was Berlin's answer to the "hijack pop" coming out of record studios these days, but Berlin's music had its own hypnotic quality that was hard to place. It forced you to feel its presence, to listen. It surprised you into attention.

It erased things, somehow, as if canceling out the lower frequencies of thought and crystalizing only what was at the surface.

Was it good? His songs were so familiar now that it was hard for you to say. You weren't Berlin's audience, anyway. You were his friend.

You swayed a little to the song as you weaved along through the crowd toward the bar. Trinity, a transplant from a now-defunct borough of exNY, was behind the bar. You liked her: she had pet cats, a pocket knife, and an attitude. There was a streak of green in her hair, piercings in her ears and eyebrows, and constellations of tattoos across her chest and face. You moved through the crowd in a haze to get to her where she stood wiping down the bar with a cloth. It was as grounding a sight as anything: you'd seen her like that a hundred times.

"Hey," you said as you came up to the bar.

"Hey."

The song ended. Berlin announced his last song of the night, and it began.

You remembered several things very quickly, so vividly it was as though the scenes were right in front of you:

1. Talking with Berlin in the RV as he played these opening notes while putting together this set list.
2. Passing a joint around Berlin's little den at a party he hosted last week while this song played.
3. Violet listening to this song for the first time with a hilarious look of horror on her face (some people just don't get Adorno).
4. 2am last year, lying awake while Berlin wrote it, a memory you had almost completely forgot.

Then you were back in the bar. The song kept going. It felt like an age had passed.

"You ok?" Trinity quirked her head at you and did her eyebrow thing.

It was difficult to say.

"Has Berlin... offered you anything?" you ventured.

"No." She crossed her arms and did her pouting thing. Trinity had lots of little quirks. "Should he have?"

"I don't know. I think... no. We need to cut this off before it gets out of control." Déjà vu—didn't you just say that?

"Cut what off?" Trinity asked, resting her chin in her hand. Another quirk, so familiar. "I like out of control."

*Cut off whatever the Hell this is,* you thought, head swimming in it.

Again, you fell through the moment. It was brief, this time, and then Berlin was right beside you, clapping you on the back.

"Send me a Supercoke," Berlin said. He turned to you. "What do you want?"

"Supercoke."

"Two Supercokes."

"I got it," Trinity said, whipping him in the head with a dishtowel.

"And you're not gonna congratulate me on my set?"

"Your music's shit, Berlin," Trinity called over her shoulder.

"I was totally transported," you said, and smiled, but your eyes were saying something else, as though someone else were seeing through them.

Berlin inclined his head toward you and lowered his voice. "You okay?"

"Not really."

"I know. This shit's got me feeling like a tangled shoelace."

You were afraid. Berlin wasn't listening. You were spinning around a whirlpool of predestination with inevitable future at its center, alternate routes flashing by under the surface of the water. Now you were out on the edge, almost out, and it was pulling back on you with all its strength.

"Berlin..."

Trinity brought the Supercokes; Berlin took them from her. He made a joking gesture as if to sip from both and then handed yours to you, presenting it with a little flourish. Trinity rolled her eyes.

*To take a sip, turn to page 192*

## 10

---

"'*A rea 51 drug?!*' Are you crazy?!"

"Fine line between madness and genius, my friend. Come on. Take a walk on the wild side."

You watched Berlin, careful. His runaway lopsided smile had a touch of mania to it, but that was not unusual for Berlin. Furthermore, he seemed to shimmer as though touched by an iridescent halo, but that could have been an effect of the twinkling string lights that lit the RV.

"But if it really is *that crazy,*" you reasoned, "I'd like to know a little more about where this thing is coming from and what's going to happen if I take it!"

Berlin's smile faded to annoyance as he rolled his eyes. "I'm not *making* you take it!"

Ah. A trump card. He was taking it off the table.

TO TRY THE DRUG, *turn to page 22*

To refuse, *turn to page 24*

# 11

It was rash, you knew. It was dangerous. But something had set a flame inside you that saw everything as interconnected, saw Berlin how he was suffering, saw the power in every little pivot point. This moment was charged with power, like you'd crossed a universe to get here, and you weren't going to waste it. Not now, while you had it in your hands.

So you'd set a fire. Let freedom ring.

You hugged Berlin goodbye. "I'm getting you out of here," you said in his ear, and he pounded you twice on the back to show his gratitude. It was hard, letting him go and leaving.

It started to rain, wind picking up something terrible. Unseasonable. And the rain would make arson more difficult. But here you were, determined. Driven by manic certainty. Fuel should do the trick. Yes.

You were driving the camper to the gas station through the rain when it happened. A man in a black hat and dark suit stepped out into the middle of the road.

You slammed on the brakes. The van hydroplaned into a skid. You closed your eyes.

TURN *to page 68*

## 12

## THE CENTER OF THE UNIVERSE

The rain lashed against the windows of the Red Arrow diner, each drop forming a fractal upon impact before hurrying away. The pattern on the floor crawled around as if there were insects beneath it. And Violet, how she glowed in the morning light.

It was all alive around you: the percolating coffee, the tinkle and clatter of silverware, the fluff coming out of the familiar red leather seat of Violet's favorite booth. Everything else faded away. There was the mirror backsplash behind the counter, the bell above the door, the rain against the windows, but beyond that rain you sensed very little. Instead, there was Violet, pensive look on her face. Your love for her like the core of the Earth.

It felt like a dream: contextless and abstract, all veiled light and feeling. You were not sure how you got here, you were just *here,* self-evident and comfortable. You felt there was something important you had forgotten. Perhaps you would remember. Perhaps it was just another forgotten thing.

To propose to Violet, *continue reading on the next page.*

*Do not open the box. Turn to page* 38

## 13

## PANDORA'S CAT

Yes. Love, true love and all that. That was how it was supposed to go, wasn't it? Love and devotion and eternal happiness. You wanted to show her you were faithful, committed, that she meant the world for you. Of course, you knew you were doomed. You knew you were doomed when you met her. And these past weeks, as she's slowly turned away from you, as you've felt that influence of her father or some general greater logic, you've known that it's now or never. You needed to grab hold before it was too late. And now, in the Red Arrow Diner, this favorite haunt where you fell in love, you would put it all on the line. Your anticipation, the thrill of foreboding, suspended you for a moment as if in midair. As if in time. This moment could last forever, before this enormous milestone of life came down one way or another.

But it could not be prolonged forever. You reached for the small blue velvet box in your bag. Your heart raced, your hands shook. You opened the box under the table, for one last glimpse to get your courage up.

But it was gone.

Your grandmother's engagement ring was gone.

Your body jumped into overdrive. Panic. Pure panic. A whirlpool of helplessness and fear swirled in your stomach. This was wrong. How did this happen? The future rushed up at you, like stopping short in traffic, trying to remind you to hit the brake, but it was too late. You were crashing. A conclusion came to you, something impossible, something half-remembered that didn't make sense, but was also the only answer. *Time travel.* It must have shown on your face, because—

"Hey, you okay?"

*To tell her everything's fine, turn to page 43*
*To confide in her, turn to page 45*

## 14

---

## THE DAMN

There was something about this box, this moment, something screaming inside you that was so, so scared. It was natural, of course, to have anxiety about a proposal. But you had made up your mind about this, hadn't you? Hadn't you laid in bed in the RV, mulling this over, concluding that it had to be done?

Something in your gut—that place beyond memory—told you not to open the box. Why? *Yes, you can almost feel it, epiphany...* But you're not sure. Just... not now. It wasn't right. You had to trust that feeling.

It stopped raining.

Your breakfast came. The bell above the door rang again as a trio of patrons shuffled out. And again. And again. It was ringing in tempo, and the rhythms and sounds of the diner were transforming into a synthesized melody...

You were back in the RV. It was raining. You were in the diner. You were in the RV.

"You said there was something you wanted to tell me?"

Violet in your ear with Berlin's hand on your shoulder. In Berlin's universe, you said: "Oh, shit, I feel sick," and doubled over. The floor of the RV was crawling with invisible insects, too. You closed your eyes.

In Violet's universe, you said: "It's nothing. I'm just happy to be with you."

She smiled blithely. "That's lovely." Then, a deadly pause. "But lately, I've been thinking..."

*Shit, this could not be happening. Not again. Not anyway.* You could feel the seam of time pulling tighter.

"Get outta there!" Berlin called. "Drop anchor somewhere closer to now!"

Time scrolled by like movie credits: wide, wide. You were back at the Qwik Mart, in the middle of a shift infinite. You lingered there. The campfire smoke familiar curled around you and clung to your clothes: *Not a winner! Not a winner! Not a winner!* Dour green presidential faces. Bright red cans of Supercoke. The cash register going beep, beep, beep, bing! with every purchase, and the drawer rolling open, rrrrrrrrrr-kch!

And then the drawer rolling open was the sound of your longboard rolling beneath you, cha-chuck, cha-chucking over gaps in the pavement, not unlike a train, and you bent your knees and watched the world slide by. Compared to the neon Qwik Mart, so vivid in your memory it was almost peripheral, the colors outside were softer and ill-defined. You noticed, now, the geometric pattern formed by the leaves, the branches, the trees as they were positioned, by the flowers, every blade of grass, even the little ions of water in the air were now perceptible to you, cool on your face as the wind rushed by. And here and there was the warm orange breast of a songbird, flitting from tree to tree, flying with you. For a fleeting moment, there was love that did not ache.

Why were you aching? That thing you weren't thinking of—it didn't exist. It never existed. And the air felt so fresh, just then, fresh and bright and possible.

You kicked at your longboard's back end and caught it from the top and tucked it under your arm so you could go for your keys. A jangling laugh as you pulled them from your bag and inserted them in the door; your pepper spray, brass knuckles, and bottle opener clinked merrily against a big plastic keychain that read "TAKE IT EASY - BUT TAKE IT! NEW ORLEANS, LA"

"Take a sip of this, it'll ground you," said Berlin. You sipped. It was just regular Supercoke. But it did ground you. "You're staying balanced. That's good. Try to stay with me a little while. Don't get sucked down too far anywhere."

"I thought I was supposed to find an anchor?"

"At first, as it settles in. Then you gotta be careful not to get carried away. Because after a certain point... let's just say there's a boundary. The border of reality. The deeper you are out there, the easier it is to cross."

You took another sip of Supercoke. It *did* ground you, in a weird way.

Berlin looked serious. "You think you can help me?"

You nodded.

"Good. I might be in a *little* bit of trouble with the people I got this shit from."

*"Berlin!"*

"Calm down. I'll be right here to help you through it."

You closed your eyes and fingered your way through your memory catalogue. OK. You could do this. Dancing visions materialized over your eyelids in impressions of the past: Violet in her favorite booth, the wave crashing in, Berlin at the wheel of the RV, flooring it, fleeing with Trinity from a crowded bar. And there was a sinking up sort of sensation as you dissolved into the memory of that afternoon, finally landing.

You, with a blunt and *Breakfast of Champions* on the sofabed (now a sofa), wondering vaguely where Berlin had gone, since shouldn't he have returned by now? Something told you you ought to be out looking for him, if only you could force yourself to remember the future.

You concentrated on moving your past self's body. Affecting it through force of will. It was not as easy as it had been when you'd begun: when it was merely a matter of sinking into the memory. Now, it was more like walking upstream. Possible, but you felt the pull. The dosage, wearing, had peaked, and you had settled into it. The visuals had calmed, though present, but its effect on you was deeper, somehow, as though you felt time passing over you through osmosis. The past, the future, wherever you weren't, went quiet. You sank into the trip and waited for the future to come.

TURN *to page 95*

## 15

---

"Everything's fine," you said. The water poured in.
Violet waved her hand in front of your face.

"Are you on drugs?"

Ha. How like her, to know. She could anticipate you in a way that approached dangerous. You were a mystery to her, once, an X factor, and that had made you exciting, intriguing. There was something to be said, of course, about familiar intimacy, but the shrewdness of her tone did not bode well.

She had that look on her face, too, disapproving and certain, worried but amused in spite of herself. These were your antics, after all. You were hers.

The rain roared and whispered. Hexagons, explosions of hexagons. You closed your eyes, and there were hexagons in your head, floating around on the back of your eyelids.

How to tell her what you might be on—how you dwelled on her, how it was leaking in? How did you tell her, *the engagement ring I wanted to give you's gone miss-*

*ing, and my future self is a suspect?* It was possible, wasn't it? Was it? How could you tell her when you know that in a previous universe, this conversation ended with you never seeing her again?

To CONFIDE IN HER, *continue reading on the next page.*
 *To tell her everything's fine, turn to page* 49

## 16

———

W here to begin? You rolled along your timeline like a marble.

There was water on the floor of the diner. A leak in the ceiling, too. You determinedly did not look at Violet. The storm was coming in, running in rivulets down the walls and sinking into your shoes. Up to your ankles, now. The raindrop fractals on the window grew larger, like fireworks. Violet didn't seem to notice. She was looking at you.

"I'm... things are getting a little out of control right now," you tried, trying to match her energy, to get caught in the intoxicating web of her attention. But something was wrong with your connection to her, glitching static like an old antennae television in a storm.

"Berlin gave me..."

The lights flickered, the world flashed around you, and you were—

In the RV:

"Take a sip of this, it'll ground you," Berlin said. Here

you were in the RV, whenever that was. You sipped. It was just regular Supercoke. But it did ground you, its gentle fizz. One. Two. Three. Each universe an olive at the end of your finger. *Look, Mom, I'm an alien!* all the way back there.

"You're losing your balance. That's bad. Don't get sucked away anywhere." Berlin grabbed your shoulder, hard. "That's how you end up on the psych ward."

The sensation of sliding back to the future hurt like the last leg of a marathon. "Fuck this, man, just let me trip."

Berlin slapped you. "*Are you hearing me?* You have to be careful. You can't stumble out beyond the boundary. Then border patrol takes over."

"'Border patrol?'"

"The edge of reality. There's this central infrastructure that'll try to keep you in. It's hard to explain. Trust me, you don't want to find out the hard way."

*All the water pouring in...*

"You got this."

You took another sip of Supercoke. It *did* ground you, in a weird way.

"Where did you go?" Berlin asked.

"This morning, with Violet..." you replied. "At least, I think it was this morning. It was the diner, whenever it was."

"Be careful," Berlin warned. "The universe seems to patch itself up, but this can get out of control fast. What happened this morning?"

"We broke up."

"F."

"Shut up."

"Sorry. What's going on back there? Are you... are you trying to change it?"

"No, I... I don't know what I... it was raining. Like, *inside.*"

"That's the boundary. It's very aqueous. We don't know why."

"'We?'"

"We in the hallucinogenic drug dealer community. We have a reddit."

You buried your head in your hands. "What the Hell is going on?"

"I mean, if you really want to know, it wasn't too hard to piece together. Time exists only when observed, right? So your memory isn't just a record, it's the very fabric upon which time travels. Right?"

You just looked at him.

"So somehow this drug expands your perception of time and allows you some limited movement within the boundaries of the dimension. I'm not sure, but our best guess is that what we change in the past resonates through reality in what our brain perceives as osmosis, because the actual process is too complicated for our tiny minds to understand."

"So we *can* change things, or we can't?"

"Unclear. Just don't break symmetry, or the universe will break you."

You let all this information simmer for a moment. Then you asked: "There's just a bunch of dealers on reddit theorizing about time travel?"

"'A bunch' is generous, but yeah, pretty much."

"Meaning, these hallucinations... they're real?"

"Unfortunately."

Then, it strikes you:

*The ring.*

Almost like you're back in the diner, looking at the empty box. Which—oh, Jesus, it catches up to you the way video sounds on rewind:

"Violet, I have a fucking time machine." You leaned across the table and took her hand in yours. Looked into her earnest, worried eyes—Violet Hunter, if you only knew...

There was a pull on you, now, as if someone had pulled a plug in the diner floor and now you were being sucked away with the water. But you could fight it, if you wanted, and hold on tighter.

To HOLD FAST, *turn to page 55*

*To take another sip of Supercoke, turn to page 56*

## 17

"Everything's fine," is what you wanted to say, but what you said was, "Violet..."

Memories of Violet swam before you, tangible, as if they were projected on the rain. Sitting with her on the sofa in her shitty little apartment, binge watching television in a haze of valentine and Supercoke. Violet laughing as you walked down the street with her in winter, wrapped in your coat. Violet settling a serious argument with a group of her friends as you lingered watchful over her shoulder; she spoke stern and emphasized her points with her finger.

And then there were memories that were not memories at all, for as far as you could tell, they had never happened: losing Violet at some sort of dark party, pushing through the crowd as you looked for her. Violet's strained scream as heard from a distance. The crackling and light from a bonfire, the drone of heavy male voices, the wail of a siren. Where were you?

The water was coming in. The diner, still the diner.

Violet across from you, now reaching over the table to grab your hand. You held on.

*T*O TELL *her you love her, to tell her everything, continue reading on the next page.*

*To let her go, turn to page 52*

*To let her go, turn to page 52*

## 18

-------

As the rain came down, you tried to tell her everything, which you experienced more as a sensation than as a coherent string of words. Time passed so fast, and yet not at all, that the moment felt more like a memory than something you lived, a smell you could remember without knowing its origin. *If you love me, you trust me, if you love me, you'll know I'm telling the truth.*

She didn't.

"That's a lot, babe," Violet replied, voice measured. "I just... have to run to the bathroom, okay? I'll be right back."

Off she went through the leaking rain, shimmering. And that was where Violet Hunter hid while the police came to take you away.

*Turn to page 59 to go to the hospital*

## 19

## ECHO PRIME

It stopped raining.

You looked around, filled with a sudden clarity. What was it you'd been worrying about again?

"Let's get out of here," Violet said, putting cash on the table for her coffee. "Something's up with you today."

There was a man in a hat in the next booth and he was watching you.

"Come on," Violet said, standing up and into the stranger's line of vision. She grabbed you by the crook of your elbow and pulled you from the booth. "You're worrying me."

"Sorry," you said, trying not to look over your shoulder as you passed into the parking lot.

"No, you don't have to—" she stopped. Pinched the bridge of her nose. Closed her eyes and smiled, prim and even. "You're fine. You're just... you."

"What's that supposed to mean?"

But you knew what it meant. Right there, right then, you saw it coming.

"It means I'm not sure I have time to worry about you, okay? I need to graduate magna cum laude or my career is dead."

"Honey, you got this."

"Easy for you to say!"

"Easy because you're a genius, Vi, not because I don't think education is important! You're amazing, and you're gonna be a great lawyer!"

"Thank you."

"You're gonna save the world! You're gonna take down big oil! You're gonna become the President of the United States!"

"Okay, shut up," she said, but smiling (real, this time).

"What will be your first act as President?"

Her eyes sparkled. "Dumping you."

Which drew you both up short—the words themselves, and the chill in the air after them.

She broke eye contact and fumbled through a weak recovery, tucking her wild dark hair behind her ear. "I'm sorry, I... I just can't do it right now, okay? I need to focus on my classes."

Your first thought was that Berlin would say that was such a stuck up tightass excuse.

"Okay, that's fine, yeah," you said. "That's fine."

"I'm gonna go back to my dorm."

"Okay."

"Bye."

"Bye."

And she walked away.

Humiliation and shame boiled in your stomach with the sadness. You watched her go.

———

This is the conclusion of the ECHOPRIME timeline of volume 1.

*T*URN *to page 1 for the story of how it all began again*

## 20

_____

"Violet," you said, bursting with urgency, her hand clutched in yours: "something terrible is going to happen to you."

You didn't know what made you say it—it was not what you had meant to say. But you were certain of it like the sky before a storm. That was all that mattered, and yet, you knew she didn't understand; you were already heartbroken by the set of her eyebrows. And that was familiar, the way it had gone before. Different but the same, sewn up.

The drain pulled on you harder.

TO SLIP AWAY, _turn to page_ 57
To explain yourself, _turn to page_ 51

## 21

———————

The diner washed away in a sparkle of carbonation as you leaned into the current and sank up. Sitting again on the sofabed in the RV, you were surprised that you weren't sopping wet.

The Supercoke was refreshing, crisp, and sweet. It fizzed in your mouth, immediate and present. It kept you here, in this room, Berlin frowning at you with a crease in his brow.

"If you haven't cottoned on by now, there are actually a few reasons why I think we'd be better off skipping town."

To PROTEST, *turn to page 153*

*To skip town, turn to page 155*

## 22

## THE CROSSROADS OF TIME

The rain on your face felt so real, the winds of the universe, the whoosh of the current as it escorted you in its strong arms to the red lights and beyond. You sank into the trip like you were sleeping, master of it now, thumbing through your past like a well-loved novel.

You cast anchor a few hours ago, early evening. You were wide going narrow with all your strength. *Just stay tight,* you thought, tensing your muscles and holding yourself as far *in* as you could. *Land.*

You were in your room. Just... *there.* Time was passing by around you in fits and bursts: first it wasn't, then it was. And you were at peace for a moment, outside of it, without all this chaos, distractions, and noise, at sea.

And then there was a knock at the door.

You paused, suspended. You really just wanted to lie here and ride out this trip; you were starting to feel very circular and sick. Dizzy, you meant. Dizzy.

It's not quite right that there's a knock at the door. That's not how it went the first time, you know. But you are not sure when you are, and what a first time really is, anyway.

There was the knock again. *That* knock.

TO ANSWER THE DOOR, *turn to page 99*

*To pretend no one's home, turn to page 103*

## 23

The diner collapsed around you like a deflating bounce house and reformed in the shape of an ambulance, all shiny metallic and tools. They had to muscle you into the stretcher, bind you down. You fought. In the end, they sedated you.

You tried to skim through it, semi-conscious. You tried to make it go away.

They held you for 3 days. For all 3 days, the windows of the institution were thick with fog. You played chess with a man named Ken. You rode the stationary bike. You hovered in suspended moments, all your outlines psychedelic at the edges. You went to group. You went to bed early.

Berlin was in your dreams.

"I figured out a way to get you out of here," he said in an undertone that rode low beneath the murmur of visiting hours. "You took it, right?"

What was the point in lying? You nodded.

"Just hop back to before you told Violet what's going on," Berlin said. "It'll be like none of this will ever happen."

To SINK UP, *continue reading on the next page.*
*To hold fast, turn to page 62*

## 24

————

"How am I supposed to get there?" you asked. It wasn't a dream, it was visiting hours. You weren't allowed too close to each other; the orderlies were watching.

Berlin, all confidence, touched his index finger to his lips, and when he took it away the little bunny-faced square was poised right at the seam of his plump lower lip. Then, before you could fully register what he was doing, he leaned in and stole a gentle peck, just enough to transfer the acid tab from his lips to yours.

You licked the tab onto your tongue.

"It was really good to see you," Berlin said. "Feel better."

SINK UP *to page* 34

## 25

"I don't know, Berlin," you said, *so* aware of your presence in *this* moment, this place where you could walk away. The hospital a harbor. You prepared yourself to remember it: visiting hours, the horrible white halls and glowing red EXIT sign and the sound of the other crazy people and their families. "Maybe this should be the end of it."

"What are you saying?"

"I don't want any part of this. It messed me up enough. I don't know what kind of shit you've gotten yourself into, but I'm getting out before I go in."

"Come on, you don't mean that."

"I do mean that. Maybe Violet is right. I'll ride out the fucking sentence. You know? Maybe I could do worse."

"Visiting hours have ended!" cried an orderly.

"Don't say that," Berlin said. "Come on, I... I really need you on this one."

He came forward and hugged you, and used that fleeting moment of contact to shove something into the front pocket of your sweatshirt.

You felt it, unmistakable: a sheet of acid tabs.

"Lin, I..."

"Just think about it, okay? I'll... I'll see you at home."

You woke up sweating, tabs in your pouch pocket, taunting you iridescent in the moonlight. *You'll talk to Berlin when you get out of here,* you told yourself, certain you could tell the difference between memory and dream.

But you didn't see Berlin when you got out. He didn't pick you up on release day, and when your cab arrived at the camper, it was abandoned. No signs of a struggle. Nothing.

You tried his phone, the number was disconnected. Checked his socials—gone black, like they never existed. And the tabs in your sweatshirt pocket were starting to cry out in Berlin's voice. Yes, they were there. Yes, you had seen him. You were afraid of it—but what other choice did you have? Let Berlin just... disappear?

TO USE THE TIME TABS, *continue reading on the next page.*

To stay here, turn to page 66

## 26

*Fuck it,* you thought, and took 5.

As you collapsed onto the sofabed, a now familiar feeling overtook you: a sort of rise, a sort of twist, a stretch and bending backwards. The colors of the world whirled rainbow as time raced by in little brackets of color and light. Patterns burst out in every direction across time and space, wriggling like ants over reality's surface. Much of your timeline did not leave this very spot, so comfortable in your small bed, but the white fluorescent hospital light bordered the edges of your vision. You were riding the stationary bike.

Perhaps, if you sunk back further, as if into a dream...?

To DREAM, *turn to page* 34

## 27

# THE OUTER LIMITS

Quiet, intentional, you took up a lighter from the table and set the sheet of acid tabs on fire. You dropped it in an empty glass and watched it curl to ash.

Then, you grabbed the keys from the visor, hopped into the driver's seat, got gas, and skipped town.

Whatever they'd done to you at the hospital, it hadn't quite worked right. You were on edge, jumpy, talked to yourself—revisiting events over and over, noting similarities, differences. Deciding on roads to take and it was *this one, this one,* riding southwest across the country like the sunset meant something to you, white knuckled with the radio on.

You could hear the future you left behind, felt it stretching taut. But you kept driving, and the tether strained and strained and strained until eventually it snapped as you took an impulsive exit off the freeway without signaling. Immediately, your seams relaxed and unraveled.

And you left it behind, and went on existing.

You hooted and cheered and banged your fist on the ceiling, filled with uncertain elation. But it felt right, like you'd just snapped the chain of something, and in your new world was a better future.

This was how you began.

———

This is the conclusion of the ECHO1 timeline of volume 1.

*T*URN *to page 1 to remember*

## 28

## THE PINKERTON WARD

You woke strapped to a hospital bed in a quiet, white room. Outside, you could hear the movement of people, the hum of chatter, the whir of machines and ringing phones. But your windowless room was sparse, unmoving, dead: the bed upon which you laid cold and unyielding, dressed with a white waffle blanket that offered no comfort or warmth.

"Berlin?" you said, turning around, testing the resistance of your bindings. "Berlin?"

He was nowhere.

You took further stock of your surroundings: your phone was gone, and thus your connection to the outside world. It could be anywhen in here, day or night, abstracted from time and space. Above you, a fluorescent light glowed, harsh against the skin like your blanket. You closed your eyes and turned away from it, struggling against your bonds.

A man entered. A man in black.

"So," he said, taking a seat in a chair that was not

there a moment before. He was examining notes on a clipboard he'd not had when he walked in. "Tell me what you have been experiencing."

You did not answer. You stared at him.

He made a note on his clipboard. There was something horrible and suffocating about him, the room, the tile floor, the fluorescent light. It seemed to shrink around you, the walls pulsing, caving in.

"Let me out."

"If you behave, I'll consider it."

*'Behave?'*

"Tell me about what happened."

To TELL HIM WHAT HAPPENED, *continue reading on the next page.*

*To remain silent, turn to page 72*

## 29

---

"I don't know," you answered, though the truth swam before you. Best to start at the beginning. "There's this drug."

"You took a drug," the doctor confirmed.

"Yeah. I don't know what it was," you lied.

"How did you ingest it?"

The bonds felt particularly tight. "Mouth."

"And how did you procure them?"

"My friend. Did you take him?"

The man did not reply, unmoved. He made another note on his clipboard. "And the effects of this drug were?"

"Tripping. Hallucinations. The usual stuff."

"'The usual stuff.'"

"Yeah."

"What sort of hallucinations?"

"Patterns. You know, visuals."

"Any time distortion?"

You tried not to smile. "A little, yeah."

"'A little.'"

"Yeah."

"Do you remember the circumstances under which you arrived here tonight?"

"Yes."

"What were they?"

It took you a long time to decide what to say. Finally: "I lost control."

"Hmm." Another note.

"What are you writing?" you asked.

"I am assessing you for a stay at our inpatient facility."

"Why? Am I crazy?"

The man veiled his reaction to this question. Then, he looked straight at you, and said, "I don't know."

He stood, approached you, and undid the topmost belt of the three that restrained you. Then, he unclipped his papers, shuffled a new one to the top, and handed the clipboard to you. "Sign this."

"What is it?"

"You need to sign it."

To SIGN IT, turn to page 74

To refuse, turn to page 76

## 30

---

"If I tell you, you'll think I'm crazy," you said.

The doctor sank into an appraising leer. His lips pursed and the corners of his eyes tightened. After a moment, he leaned back in his chair at greater ease, as if he'd found something in you which satisfied.

"If you are able to tell me this, that is all I need to know." He had the heavy accent of a native Russian speaker. "Your friend is in detox at present. He will join us here when he is ready."

"...Where's 'here?'"

"'The Pinkerton ward at Clearview Hospital. Are you having trouble remembering anything else about yourself? What is your name?"

The question surprised you. It was not 'who are you,' a more nebulous concept that yet you knew with greater confidence. It was specific, historical, it attached you to places and people and things. You were different names to different people. And what did this doctor want with your name?

And yet, already too much time had passed since he had asked and you failed to answer. With every passing microsecond his face fractioned through phases of increased severity and the room was pushing in so silent and suffocating and yellow with the files stacked high high high

and you told him your name.

"Fine, that is not so hard, see? I will talk to you tomorrow. Take your medication."

And then you were dismissed.

*T*URN *to page 8o*

## 31

You signed. The doctor undid the rest of your restraints.

"Thank you for your cooperation. I'll have the nurses by shortly to bring you upstairs."

A flash of Bob Smith on the doctor's face as he bowed out of the room—a smile.

The door closed. You went to it—locked.

Though you were alone, you felt the walls were watching you. You were doing everything you could to contain yourself, hold it together, obedient and check-book balanced. And it wasn't working. The walls were whispering to each other, the sky was red. One wall said to another, *look at this one, it can hear us.* Perhaps there was nothing you could do. Perhaps you'd gone crazy.

Of course, if you are reading this, you know what it was I was feeling that day. It was you. Reading this. My living memory pressed to paper, preserved and stretched, defaced and smiling. For you. So you might understand I was a time traveler. Here I am again in the past, waving to you. Wish you were here.

There is so much more I want to tell you. Central, Shibboleth, the cloud giants. My dreams. But I am wary. I am not often believed, you see. Become too emphatic and I risk a return visit to an institution much like the one from which this narrative has just departed. When you are in a situation like mine, you satisfy yourself by watching *12 Monkeys* with Trinity. You laughed and drank wine and Trinity kept calling it "a *divine* comedy" and holding a glass of red like she was so clever. It was still the end of the world.

*To* REMEMBER *how you got out of the hospital, turn to page* 87

## 32

—————

"Why?"

"Everything will be easier if you do."

"Easier for who. You?"

"We're asking for your consent."

"To stay on the ward upstairs?"

"Yes."

"I don't want to stay on the ward upstairs."

"Yes, but this will make it easier."

You did not sign.

The man took his clipboard and left. Your legs were still strapped to the bed.

The nurses came in with a wheelchair. You fought to get up, to escape —but there were four of them, one of you, and a needle. Sufficiently threatened, you put up no resistance.

They wheeled you through the hospital. No windows. You did not pass the sliding doors to reality. The universe was long white halls and fluorescent light.

"You'll have to give us your shoes," said the nurse, "and any personal items."

"My shoes?"

"And any personal items. We already have your phone."

"What have you done with it?"

"We'll store it. With your shoes."

"I don't consent to be here!"

They gave you the piece of paper on the clipboard again. They set the wheelchair right up in front of a long poster in legalese with the heading "KNOW YOUR RIGHTS."

"Just sign it, it will be easier," the nurses said.

You read your rights. They could keep you here against your will for three days, it seemed, not counting weekends and holidays (which should have counted, you thought). If you had signed the document, you would have been volunteering to stay indefinitely.

"Just sign it," the nurses said. "It will be easier."

They kept you awake, wheeling you from brightly lit place to brightly lit place, asking you to sign. They tried to make you shower, which you refused, though they did force you out of your shoes, personal belongings, and favorite jacket. Locked away.

Then it was morning. They took you to your doctor. He was a large man: heavy, with sunken eyes and a heavy slavic accent. He had a shiny gold DOCTOR KOZLOV nameplate on a desk overflowing with stacks of forms and files. "They say you will not sign the section 12."

You said nothing.

"You should do this. Everything will be easier if you sign."

You crossed your arms. "You can only hold me for 3 days."

"Then, we go to court. And I will make my case to the judge about why you should remain in hospital care. It is very difficult and time consuming for everyone. It can take a long time. You think you can win this case?"

It was as though a bit of acid had been released from a crack in your hippie spine: the visuals came flooding back in a whirlpool to the brown brown future, a stranglehold of cell walls rigid and rectangular. You were on the stand in a straitjacket, this bored and disaffected doctor barely looking up from his notes.

"You sign the section 12, you are cooperating with hospital procedure, if you behave, I will volunteer to let you out in 3 days. Everything easier. While you know the courts. It takes time even to get in."

"You can't keep me until then."

"You think I will let you out? You may be a danger to yourself and society. It is my duty as a doctor to keep you here. You are making my job very difficult."

You narrowed your eyes at him. "You'll let me out in 3 days?"

"Well, 5. There is a holiday."

"And you can't just... let me out?"

"We don't release patients then," Kozlov said, calm, eyes on a paper on his desk. "You see how it benefits you to make this as easy as possible? I do not want to fight you. I want to *help* you."

Why did so many people seem to say that?

The dread future was seceding like low tide, and you knew why. It was less threatening. You had no choice.

*TURN to page 87 to sign the section 12*

## 33

---

# THE DOORS

There were 3 doors to the hall where there should have been 1, and they were all slightly overlapping. The sight of it made you dizzy, but it clarified the Wonderland lunacy you'd been feeling about this horrible place, like everything was melting. It was more than just a feeling. You were lost.

To take the door on the right, turn to page 84

To aim for the door in the middle, turn to page 83

To choose the door on the left, continue reading on the next page.

## 34

---

You went through the first door and you were all in group sitting in a circle on these shitty fucking chairs and there were people in this room like you couldn't fucking believe, alcoholics with dead children and a woman being stalked by the mafia and an honest to God giant who'd just given up his quest for revenge for the death of his twin brother. And here you were sitting there knowing you couldn't tell them you've got a fucking time machine. *Jeeeeeesus.*

And then you were in the same room and the lights were off and your doctor was in there and state representatives and there was a light on you and they were assessing you to see if you were crazy and you couldn't tell them you've got a time machine and you agreed with everything the doctor said. Here you were agreeing to stay in the hospital. Here you were.

But the experience was so horrible you used all your might to astral project out of it, dwell in your memories, dream of your revenge. Anything to escape the whiteness of the walls, the murmur of conversation, the outbursts of screaming, the drone of the radio.

You were so relieved when it was time to retire to your stiff and narrow bed. There was a window in your room, but it looked out to a brick wall. It was bliss to sleep.

YOUR DREAM IS *on page 34*

## 35

The middle, you reasoned, was the most sensible option, caught as it was between either extreme. Tipsily, you took a confident step through it, but as you did so, everything spun. You stepped not into the waiting hallway, but back into the Doctor's office. Doctor Kozlov was shuffling some papers around on his desk and did not so much as glance up at you.

The three doors stood in front of you, open, almost shimmering.

Go Left, *turn to page 81*

*or Right? Continue reading on the next page.*

## 36

You passed through the 3rd door and found yourself in a clearing outside at night. You turned around: doctor's office. You looked ahead: Field. With a bonfire.

Doctor's office—
The little cubicle of light flickered and disappeared.

You out in a hostile clearing wearing hospital pajamas.

"Shit."

The lights went out.

Lying in the stiff and narrow bed at the institution. There was a window in the room. Through the window was a brick wall.

You closed your eyes and laid back down on the bed, trying to will back your hallucination. For a moment, you could smell the night air, hear crickets—but when you opened your eyes: darkened hospital room.

You heard the crackling of fire. You lifted your head from the pillow. There, or here?

Before you could determine this, the silhouette of a man in a familiar hat appeared in the doorway.

"We got off on the wrong foot," he said.

You stiffened.

"I brought you something."

"..What?"

He pulled from his jacket pocket a small, rectangular piece of paper. It was unmistakably a sheet of time tabs. He held it pinched between his middle and forefinger and gave it a jaunty little wave. "This is an offer, not a sample."

"Offer of what?"

"Berlin's gun. It's your beginning and end. Do you know that?"

Strange question. You didn't answer.

Small chuckle from Bob. "The ring, genius."

"What?"

"The ring. We're in the timeline where you don't

open the box that morning. Schrödinger's suspension, you see? You can still stop him from stealing it."

You said nothing.

"He pawned it. For the gun. Or have you known, and just not cared? The loyalty is sweet, really. But there are bigger things out there."

"Go to Hell."

"Ttch tch ch," Bob said. "That's something I like about you, you know. That's why I'm standing here right now."

"That I want you to go to Hell?"

"That you don't see the institution for the opportunity it represents," said Bob. *"Comprende?"*

You grit your teeth.

"Take these." He gave them to you. "You don't have to hurt your friend. But Central would like to show you that it rewards loyalty much better than pawning your prized possessions behind your back."

To agree with Bob, *turn to page 91*

*To distrust Bob, but take the tabs anyway, turn to page 93*

## 37

# THE TALKING MIRROR

After that you were escorted to the day room by a smiling nurse in padded shoes. You wrenched your arm out of her grasp. Don't touch my arm.

There was a radio nestled out of reach on top of a cupboard playing the most popular radio station, all pop songs that encourage drinking and have that *twang* in it. There were 3 long plain grey tables in one half of the room with some government issue lounge furniture on the other. Patients shuffled around, orderlies stationed around the room like points on a compass. A man in the corner sat alone at a chess table. Two older women and a young man frowned over a bird puzzle on another. Someone drew in a notebook, someone read the bible, someone stared dead-eyed into middle distance on a stationary bike.

There was a little kitchen, too, with a fridge and a bowl full of apples, tucked away by an outcropping of wall. The walls were bare but for some hand-made art the inpatients had taped up. Still the radio was playing, still with that insufferable *twang*. There was a mural behind you, above the entrance, a hideous one the ward would have been better off without. It was the kind you'd find in an elementary school, the kind painted by the students and conceptualized by a sub-par art teacher, with rainbow-colored silhouettes that looked more like murder victims and words like "Love" "Respect" and "Empathy" hand-detailed in the font family comic sans.

"Are you hungry?" the orderly asked.

Ignoring her, you grabbed an apple out of the bowl on the counter and went to sit with the man at the chessboard.

He was balding, but the gray hair that remained had Einsteinian endurance and capacity, sticking out and tangled. He was thin, and narrow in the way that you could tell that when he stood, he'd be tall.

"Can I sit here?" you asked, across from him.

He nodded, held his hand out to indicate the chair. "Ken," he said.

You sat down.

"Do you know how to play?" he asked.

You were on the side of the black pieces. I know how to play, so we played.

See, I have this theory about chess, which is really more of a theory of everything. But with chess it's particularly fun, since the characters are kings and queens and knights etc., and humans always like playing at those. My theory is that chess can be used as a form of divination on micro and macro levels, from the relationship between you and your partner to the battleground of the world. As you might expect, it was around this time that I was developing this theory, and I was excited to see it put to work.

Things like this happened:

The white bishop took the black knight.

The black queen took both white bishops.

The white and black kings castled.

The white knight cornered the black king behind his pawns,

Checkmate.

Would you like to play again?

That's my problem, I see patterns where I shouldn't. They put me away for doing such a thing. And when they put me away, I met other people that could do it. Isn't that funny? I met a giant. I met Derek, who thought he was dead. I met BoBo, who had seen the end of the world. Like me.

All that's coming.

But first you were locked up and you were cleansed and you were medicated, and the fog cleared, and a newspaper came, and that newspaper told you what you knew all along: that the world was ending, and there was nothing you could do. Reality was stable, and you had not gone anywhere at all. The hospital, once floating in the fog of the fifth dimension, had landed, home again.

Berlin was there. "Just fine, just fine, just came out of detox, what are you looking at me like that for?"

Nothing.

When the nurses weren't looking, in an undertone: *"Do you need to go back for something?"*

It was a hard question. A few days sober, it was hard to want to go back. To invite the beast in again. After how it ended?

But, perhaps, that was the trouble. After how it ended, why not go back? Fix it? Take a more tolerable timeline. Pick up those pieces of memory that you know have leaked out.

The missing pieces. That was the hardest part. Were they out there, wondering what happened to you?

It would drive you crazy. You'd find a way to go back and pick up every single one. And you'll do what I did.

You'll go straight through it.

———

This is the conclusion of the ECHO2 timeline of volume 1.

*T*URN *to page 1 to begin again*

## 38

---

You stared at the acid sheet.

"I could help you join the agency," Bob said. "Get you out of that RV. Get you some money. Get you out of this place, for starters." He knocked on the door frame.

"What about Berlin?"

"What about him? I said you don't have to hurt him. Just keep him from hurting me."

"But what's going to happen to him?"

"Hell if I know, he's your friend."

You thought about this for a moment. "What happens to this reality?"

"Hopefully nothing, as long as we're using it. When we're not, what's it matter where it goes?" He tipped his hat. "It's all a matter of perspective."

Then he was gone.

That thing started happening at the edges of your vision that had happened before: even before you'd taken it, the effects had started leaking in. Oh, it was almost sickening, the way it swam, that same feeling of sinking up you'd been suspended in before. *Just take it, just do it* —and you already had.

You fell forward onto all fours and the room spun. You collapsed onto your side, hugged your knees to your chest, and squeezed your eyes shut, and suddenly you were absolutely nowhere, floating in a sea of black.

You just wanted to go home you just wanted to go home you just wanted to go home.

TO DO YOUR MISSION, *turn to page 95*

*To go home, turn to page 34*

## 39

Well, he gave it to you, didn't he? Fuck it.

You ripped off a square of four tabs and dropped them on your tongue.

Bob nodded. "We will be generous if you are able to help us. When we have time, I can explain to you how little is more noble than our cause. Understanding that is part of growing up..."

You flipped Bob the bird.

Bob rolled his eyes. "Fine! Waste your time..."

You could feel yourself torn in two, almost literally, by your trust or lack thereof.

The drug was rolling in fast. The walls were wibbling, the bed felt soft and palatial, the barren room glittering with the emergence of psychedelic regalia. You could linger in this moment, if you wanted to, dwell on this conversation with Bob, piece it out, but you didn't want to. You wanted to get far away from here. You wanted to forget this ever happened. You wanted that blissed out feeling of sinking up, skating backwards, flying like a kite, and you're sure you took enough acid to do it...

CONTINUE READING *on the next page.*

## 40

### SINKING UP

Lying on your little sofa, tripping, was a good, familiar feeling. You had passed many hours in this little cocoon of space, and this was just another. Was Berlin here? How was he? Did it matter?

Then, there was something at the door. A knock at the door. *That* knock at the door. And if you were less high, you'd be more confused, because seriously, that *never fucking happens.* But hasn't it also happened before?

An inevitable curiosity drew you through the iridescent haze and down the hall, a little unsteady getting up from the sofa. You balanced yourself on the walls, which, claustrophobic at the best of times, seemed to be almost caving in. And as you walked, you felt as if on a treadmill, pulled backwards as the world slipped by.

You finally kicked open the door from the top of the stairs to find a nondescript man in a dark suit, dark glasses, and a black hat in your parking lot. In his left hand he carried a black briefcase with a silver combination lock.

"Bob Smith," he said. "Have we met?"

*If you have met Bob, turn to page 118*

*If you have not met Bob, continue reading on the next page.*

## 41

___

## BOB SMITH

Dizzy with hallucinogen, you narrowed your eyes at him. "No. Don't think so. Should I know you?"

Bob returned the hat to his head, reached into his front suit pocket, and withdrew a business card. When he held it out to you, you saw that he had the suit of spades tattooed on the inside of his wrist.

The business card read:

BOB SMITH
Balance Management Agent
*Central Infrastructure Agency*

"It has come to my attention that something went wrong in your timeline somewhere upstream. Caused quite a nasty tangle. Dam, as we know it in the industry. I've come up from the estuary to help set things straight. Understand?"

"...How did you find me?"

Bob sighed, and if you could have seen behind his

dark sunglasses, you're sure he was rolling his eyes. He pushed passed you and entered the RV, placing his briefcase in the passenger seat.

"As if CIA agents can't use reddit."

"That wasn't—"

"I've been in touch with your future self. You'll continue to cooperate, if you know what's good for you."

"'What's good for me?' As in let strangers into my home and let them go through my stuff?"

"Yes, that, precisely. Now tell me: where's the hotel?"

To protect Berlin, *turn to page* 101

*To help Bob, turn to page* 109

# 42

## THE OUTSIDER

You made your way down the hallway—wibbly hallway, wibbly floor, and down the short stairwell, which seemed canted, angled, steps too far apart and too close together.

You opened the door.

There was a man in a dark suit, dark glasses, and black hat standing there. He tipped his hat to you. In his other hand he carried a black briefcase with a silver combination lock. "Where's the hotel?"

You blinked at him. Something in your gut tried to remind you that there was more to this question than you initially supposed, that this man was more than a misled stranger, but it was like déjà vu: there was no source to the feeling, only ominous portension. You kept your face blank. "This is a campground."

The man smiled. There was something so strange and unsettling about him, and it wasn't the way the LSD made him ripple, and it wasn't the memories that weren't quite there. It was his expression: confident and superior.

His face, too, was familiar but unplaceable, and so indistinct you felt yourself forgetting him even as he smiled at you with all his teeth in the early evening dusk.

"Bob Smith," he said. "Have we met?"

IF YOU HAVE MET *Bob before, turn to page 121*
*If you have not met Bob, turn to page 97*

## 43

---

"Why would I tell you that?"

"Because I am your one and only hope of getting out of this mess alive. The sooner you understand that, the longer this timeline lasts."

"No offense, but just from my perspective, intruders in my home also seem to be a significant threat to my life. In this timeline, or any."

"Don't joke about things you don't understand."

"I'm not joking."

Bob allowed himself a smirk. "Do you trust yourself?"

Tough question.

"I'll let you sit with that one a while. But if you do, I'll be waiting." He flashed his business card again, then put it down, face-up on the nearest surface.

And he left. Painless. Something in your gut warned you it wouldn't always be that way.

You got out your phone and texted Berlin.

You

*hey, what the hell you get us into?*

Berlin

*Worth it. Trust me*

You SIGHED. Berlin was so annoying, in the good kind of way.

You sank back down onto the couch and tried to relax. Tried to calm and steady your breathing, tried to appreciate the pulsing visuals and textures crawling over your vision. But the novelty was losing its effect, and, after Bob, was starting to feel itchy. Dangerous. Like you had to keep checking over your shoulder, to nothing there, nothing there. Nothing there.

You tried to lose yourself in that timeless, cozy place you'd been in before Bob arrived... until that was the *exact place* in time you had manifested, the sun scrolling backwards so the shadows waltzed across the floor.

He knocked again, moment rewound. You laughed. You couldn't help it.

*T*URN *to page 99 to answer the door*
*To ignore it*, continue reading on the next page.

## 44

## THE TRINITY GLITCH

You waited—and then there was nothing. Silence. The knocks did not persist. Time stretched out longer, longer, leaving you in suspense—still nothing. The stranger disappeared as if he never existed. You almost forgot he had been there at all.

You contented yourself with staring at the patterns on the ceiling, crawling and swirling like so many ants. If you reached out and touched it, it may have moved, like water. You floated there, pleasantly suspended. And then someone was knocking again. You froze, convinced a threat had returned. Had it been an hour or an age?

"Come on, douchebag! I didn't come all the way out here for you to not answer the door!"

You raised your head. Trinity?

"What are you gonna do, make us stand out here until we catch up to ourselves? Come on, I know you're in there!"

Yes, it was Trinity. Your heart skipped a beat, confused, excited, and relieved.

You got up and answered the door. Trinity was supporting Berlin with his arm thrown around her shoulders; his head hung so you couldn't see his face.

"Jesus, what took you? Were you asleep? Or are you tripping too?"

"I'm tripping," you said, almost dizzy with it. You stepped aside to let her in.

"*Christ,*" Trinity said, rolling her eyes as she dragged Berlin in behind her. You grabbed his other shoulder as they came in, and together you lowered him onto the sofabed, where he slumped over onto his side. "At least you seem sane. This one showed up at my door just talking nonsense. He said I couldn't go to his show tonight unless I wanted to suffer a sudden, violent death."

Berlin had a show tonight? When was 'tonight?' You tried to think of a normal way to ask this while Trinity continued:

"When I tried to tell him everything was fine he fucking lost it. I just had to ride it out. Almost called the cops again, and you know how much he loved that. But after about an hour he just kind of collapsed."

"Yikes."

"A 'thank you, Trinity' would be nice."

"Thank you, Trinity."

"Mhmm. He perked up on the subway just enough to tell everyone about Armageddon. We were having a ball."

On the sofa, Berlin groaned.

"Go easy on him. This shit is not fucking around."

"Yeah, no kidding. I don't think you can be giving this shit out to people, ethically. You know what I'm saying?"

You stared at her. Did *she* know what she was saying?

"Do you know what it does?"

"Yeah, it turns your brain into spaghetti, I'm not a fucking idiot!"

*To THANK Trinity and pay for her train fare home, turn to page 116*

*To THANK Trinity and pay for her train fare home, turn to page 116*

*To encourage Trinity to try the drug, continue reading on the next page.*

## 45

———

"Trin, it's so much more than that."

"Don't you start."

"When do I ever help Berlin with a sales pitch? This shit is different. I'm seeing everything. It's how I've made it all the way out here."

"Honey, I don't know how else to explain this to you."

"You'd believe me if you tried it," you said. "I wouldn't have believed it. Come on." You reached into your pocket for the folded page of acid tabs. "Try it for yourself."

"*Please* not you too. I've seen enough!"

"Trinity, listen. I don't know what's happened. I don't know what you think you know. But whatever Berlin's been telling you... he might not be crazy."

"*Bob's coming,*" Berlin muttered, tossing around on your sofabed. "*Bob's coming.*"

Trinity put her hands on her hips and did her pouting thing. "Okay. Let's start there. Who's Bob?"

Tough question. "You don't want to know."

"Try me."

"He's from Central," Berlin said before you could answer. "And he wants my head."

"'Central,'" Trinity said, skeptical yet patient.

"Listen, Trin," you tried. "This drug we took—it can alter reality."

Trinity laughed.

"Okay, babe."

"You have to try it."

"I'm not trying—whatever this is, fucking *bath salts*—"

"They're not bath salts!" Berlin cried, mustering up the core strength to rise to your level before collapsing backwards again.

"I didn't believe it either," you said. "Not at first. And I'm not—I'm not gonna make you see it. I'm not going to let this timeline unravel anymore than it already has. But if we're going to fix this, you're going to have to suspend your disbelief a little. I'm seeing in, like, at least six different directions in time right now."

"Six whole directions, huh?"

You shook your head. Here it was, happening: a shadow of Bob loomed in your periphery, asking you where he could find the drugs. *Shut him out,* you told yourself, trying to look away from him. *Shut him out.*

He had his hand in your hair, pulling.

"Tell me where it is," he snarled, his voice so clear and quiet, his breath hot in your ear. "This ends now."

You gasped and fell to all fours at Trinity's feet as you wrenched from his grasp, clinging to the reality where you left him waiting on your doorstep, hidden and not-at-home. Trinity was rubbing your back, sunk to a crouch.

"Jesus, are you okay? Maybe I *should* take you two to the hospital..."

TO GO TO THE HOSPITAL, *turn to page 111*

*To tell Bob where to find the hotel, continue reading on the next page.*

## 46

"He keeps his stash in the heat register below his bed," you said, feeling time shift underneath you. Memories slipped away, as if your brain were a long hallway with doors to alternate timelines slamming shut.

Bob smiled, confident and easy. "All good things to those who cooperate," he said, and bent to examine the heat register. It was loose from all the times Berlin had removed and replaced it, and he pried it off easily. He peered inside.

"There's nothing here."

In your mind's hallway, a door creaked open down the very end. A shaft of yellow light shone through. You looked away from it.

So the drugs were gone. The air soured with Bob's disappointment, but he continued to look at you with an unsettling grim smile. Your trip darkened, sinister, foreboding. Should you have trusted this man? Did you have any choice? Should you dash now for that ray of light coming in through the crack, never to return?

Where was Berlin? Was he safe? Had you warned him about this—you or someone like you, who existed in another version of today? Last night? Tomorrow?

You bent over and held your head in your hands, half to hide yourself from the dizzying haze of reality, half to get away from Bob's unfaltering smile.

"It's alright, kid," he said in a voice that shouldn't have been soothing. "You're with me, now. Everything's going to be okay. Now, think: where's the hotel?"

What were you supposed to do? Berlin kept you out of his business for this exact reason. You closed your eyes. Some of the doors of memory were creaking open, closer, this time. Somehow you understood that Bob wanted you to peer into them, look around, to find Berlin and where he'd run.

"Well?"

There were acid tabs in your pocket, you remembered. A sheet Berlin gave you at the start of all this. What if you handed them over, would that suffice? Alternately, what if you took a tab? Should you steal away from Bob, fade into contraband ether? Would that even work?

And just like that: two doors. Ahead of you, now, instead of behind. You opened your eyes and looked up to Bob, whose smile had faded, expression curious.

TO TAKE *the acid in your pocket, turn to page* 115
    *To give the acid to Bob, turn to passage* 212

# 47

---

"Yeah, you know? I think it might be better if we wait it out at the hospital."

"No," Berlin cried. "*Not* the fucking hospital!"

"You're not exactly in the position to make that call, big man," Trinity said, wry smile on her face. She looked up at you. "I'm glad you said that. It takes a mature person to be able to make that call."

You shrugged. "You're just hyping me up."

"Maybe I am. Berlin's had me scared shitless."

"I'm sorry."

"Not your fault. But thanks. You okay?"

"I am now. Can you drive?"

Trinity gave you a gentle punch on the arm. "Course I can."

Berlin was curled up on the couch, in fluent conversation with himself. He kept turning back and forth from one hand to the other, addressing each in turn.

"How much did he take?" you asked.

"No idea. What about you?"

"Not too much," you dodged.

Trinity pushed the button to start the ignition, which struggled to turn over, sputtering. She swore, persisted, finger pressed determinedly against the button, and the RV came to life.

"It's okay, Trin, you can say I'm on bath salts," you said, trying to diffuse the tension in her shoulders. "I know this sounds crazy. Maybe you don't want to be involved. But I know you hate to miss out. And this is something." You were searching for a way to show her, sorting through you memories as if through a file cabinet, pausing here and there to look a moment over, never quite landing on something that felt plausible and right. How can you prove the existence of the invisible?

"Why don't I... change this... fucking... timeline... so I was never... fucking... in it..." Berlin muttered, crawling off the sofabed and into his bedroom. Trinity snorted a little laugh and you shared it with her.

Smile fading, you looked out into the passenger rear view mirror. You saw something.

It was a black car, boxy, flat-topped, nondescript, with a shiny silver bumper. Its license plate was black emblazoned with the name "BOBSMITH" in white letters. A grim man in sunglasses and a dark hat was driving.

"Trin?"

"Hm?"

"Floor it, maybe?"

"Floor it? Do you really think Berlin needs—?"

"No—yes—just floor it!"

It started to rain.

Trinity reluctantly increased the camper's speed, and BOBSMITH pulled right up alongside her and gave you a firm nudge that started the van off fishtailing.

Trinity increased your speed. "What the fuck is wrong with this guy?!"

"He's evil incarnate, Trin, that's what I've been trying to tell you!" said Berlin as he emerged from the back of the van with an acid tab on his tongue. "And he wants me dead! But don't worry—I'm going to fix everything."

'Fixing everything' apparently entailed collapsing backwards onto the sofabed and staring up at the ceiling, mumbling to himself. Trinity had regained control of the van and was gaining speed.

But BOBSMITH was not far behind, ramming the vehicle all along its left side as it passed. The RV slammed into the guardrail, pots and pans fell from the cabinets, dishes from the table and other detritus. Trinity swore. Berlin was shouting that he was trying to focus. And you were holding on for your life, eyes screwed up, somehow both cemented in the moment and floating up above it, looking down.

The rain fell much heavier now, so much so that water was gathering on the road. One last ram from BOBSMITH and you were hydroplaning, drifting sideways, holding your arms up in anticipation of impact—

Turn *to page 68*

## 48

———

You reached into your pocket. He saw what you were about to do just before you did it, and he started toward you, but he didn't have time. You were ahead. You were making a break for it. You staggered backwards down the hall, turning, heading for the door as you placed the tab on your tongue, planning to run, just run, run until you disappeared.

You didn't get that far. Perhaps it was your panic, your will to disappear. Perhaps it was the way you were already tripping, turned around and lost inside the sea of your own consciousness. However it happened, suddenly you were falling backward, endless, like when it happens in a dream. Bob was behind you, fingers grasping, but you struggled forward, found a door, and slammed it shut.

You were in the diner.

Return to page 34

# 49

"Yeah, I know, I'm an idiot," you said. "You know how I am with the free samples. But I'm almost down, you can leave Berlin with me, honest. We'll sleep off the trip and be ready for the show tonight. Yeah? Let me pay your train fare."

"You're gross," Trinity said, shoving your shoulder. "Be a little less of an asshole, please."

You send the digital transfer with the swipe of your finger. "It's done. I'm sorry you got wrapped up in this shit, Trin, we owe you one. I'll watch over Berlin til he's better."

"Thanks. The Armageddon comments—that really got me. I just feel like... you're not supposed to talk about that, you know?"

"I know, I know. The doctors said it's a manifestation of anxiety. He'll be fine." This was true.

And then: on the preface of sneaking by you, Trinity leaned in and kissed you on the cheek. Your face went hot where her lips touched it.

"Thanks, friend," she said, shielding her face with a veil of hair. "I know."

And she was gone.

Time passed. You didn't move.

Berlin groaned. "Ugh. What day is it?"

"Fuck if I know."

"Yeah, that's the feeling. You've taken it?"

"Yeah."

"Yeah." Berlin squeezed his eyes shut and rubbed his temples. "My head hurts like a *bitch*."

"Mine's not so bad," you replied. "I think it's wearing off."

"I took a shitton," said Berlin. "I keep ending up in the hospital."

"Shit."

"Yeah. Can you help get me out?"

Now that felt familiar.

Berlin handed you a sheet of acid tabs.

"How much do I have to take?" you asked.

"Not as much as me," Berlin said. "You can't lose it like I did. Then we'd both get locked up. But I think if you really focus, you can control the time you awaken in. So you might want to just... take a little and practice that." He *heff*ed a laugh. "We got time."


To take *a small amount and sink up, turn to page 57*

*To help Berlin escape the hospital, turn to page 161*

## 50

---

"Yeah," you said, remembering him, holding on to all of it, feeling it rush through your fingers like water, but holding on. "Yeah, we have. I've got some questions, believe it or not."

"And me? I've got answers. I'm the man with the plan. But nobody gets anything until I get what I need, and what I need now is your complete cooperation."

"What do you want?"

"6 months ago, two scientists at a top secret military lab in New Mexico absconded with a briefcase full of experimental drugs. They were found dead 2 weeks later in a Texas hotel near the border. The trail of temporal devastation left in the wake of this leak leads right to this here podunk little camper. Fancy that."

You let him in.

You felt dizzy, you were seeing three of everything.

Bob laughed. "You're in quanta. Don't you see? It doesn't matter. I've already won."

"That's what you think."

Berlin appeared from behind the curtain to his bedroom. Now, he stood tall, with a gun pointed right at Bob Smith.

"Don't make do this," Berlin said.

"You don't have it in you. Reality's on my side. I'm sorry you got messed up in this, kid, but put the gun down before somebody gets hurt."

"Stay away from me and my friends!" shouted Berlin, pulling the trigger.

The gun jammed.

Bob laughed harder.

"Fuck this" said Berlin, pulling on the trigger again without success before tossing it aside and swinging a punch in Bob's direction.

Bob dodged.

"Maybe your gun knows you made a dirty deal," Bob taunted. "Schrödinger's asshole, so to speak."

Berlin took a flying dive at Bob and made to tackle him. And Bob, in the narrow space, seemed to somehow flatten himself down to nearly shadow. Berlin came crashing into you and knocked you to the floor of the den.

"Give me the acid," Smith snarled, advancing on you.

To HELP BERLIN, *turn to page* 123
To surrender, turn to page 126

## 51

You were split into pieces, reality reflected in the shards of a broken mirror. Each iteration of yourself was distinct, conscious, but bits of each timeline overlapped, clashed, contrasted: doubled and skewed. You hovered uncertain in this moment, stretching back to your spot on the sofabed, and ahead, into uncertain conflict. Even your memory of Bob, the indistinct face in the business suit, shimmered, nebulous and vague. Had you seen him in the diner? Had you seen him *here?* And why did you feel you trusted him, as though he were a teacher you had spent many months with?

"Yeah," you said, pushing away the doubt, sticking instead with the confidence of familiarity. "Yeah, we've met."

Bob seemed to sense your insecurity and smiled. "Good," he said. He pressed his palm to the door and pushed his way inside. "If you know me, then you know what's best for you, and if you know what's best for you,

you know what's best for Berlin, and Violet, and reality itself."

Dread at the thought of Violet being pulled into this. "What do you know about Violet?"

Bob placed his briefcase on the passenger seat and made his way down the narrow hall, opening all the cabinets and hutches and inspecting under blankets, papers, clothes, and other clutter. "More than you. And the longer it stays that way, the safer she will be."

What?

He entered Berlin's little den at the end of the vehicle. "You're young. Love comes and goes. I told you not to get lost in the wild. Now: *where's the hotel?*"

*To* TELL *him you don't know anything, turn to page 124*

*To tell him what you know, turn to page 109*

## 52

---

B ob rounded on you before you could touch him. "Stay out of this, kid! Do you even realize what's at stake here? What you're messing around with?"

"They don't know shit," Berlin said, pushing himself up from the floor. "Leave them out of this. It's me you want." Hands shaking, he lifted the gun again.

"That won't save you," Bob replied. "Nothing will."

Berlin cocked the gun and pulled the trigger: still nothing.

"Come quietly, Mr. Halifax," said Bob. "I can show you a world you've never even imagined."

TO STRIKE *Bob over the head with a beer bottle, turn to* page 132

*To stay out of it, turn to page 137*

## 53

———

"I don't know where it is."

You stared at each other.

"We both know that's a lie."

You stood your ground.

"All I want," Bob said, "is a little peace." There was a blade in his hand, and the tattoo on his wrist had changed to a bright red heart. "Why is that so hard for people like you?"

You stumbled backwards. "I don't know! I—!"

Just then, the door opened, and Berlin burst inside.

"Stay the fuck away from us," he said, brandishing a gun in his hands.

"Berlin! What the—"

"Get behind me!" He wrestled himself in front of you, hand wrapped protectively around your waist. "All right, Bob, you fascist fuck. What we're gonna do's real easy. First, you're gonna walk outta here real slow."

Bob raised his hands to a placating height, palms out in a plea of innocence. He held the blade of his knife tucked into his thumb, running along his index like a splint. And if you were paying attention, you'd have noticed that the tattoo on his wrist had changed again, a curling black spade. "You have no idea what you're getting involved in."

"I think I might," Berlin said, gun trained on Bob.

"Take it easy," Bob said, lowering his hands ever-so-slightly. "Red, I'm pleased to see you. I just have a few questions. There's no need to resort to violence."

"Don't call me 'Red,'"

"You prefer Mr. Halifax?"

"Drop the knife!"

"Afraid of a knife at a gunfight?"

"Drop it."

But Bob stepped faster, now, with more authority, and he did not drop the knife.

"Run," said Berlin.

To RUN, *turn to page* 130

*To stand your ground, turn to page* 134

## 54

## DEEP WEB

You jumped to your feet and backed away, hands up.

"Bob—"

"You got answers, kid? Cause I've got some questions."

"Oh *fuck*," said Berlin, "he's calling you 'kid' now?"

"Forget the casualty you dragged into this!" barked Bob. "Your little Schrödinger's paradox has ripped a hole in the timestream 3 decades wide!" He lowered his glasses to get a better look at Berlin, who had not left the floor.

You're hopeless, you're scared: "Lin, just help him. Maybe he can help us."

"I *want* to help you," said Bob. "I don't like the alternative, Mr. Halifax, I really don't."

"Is that a threat?"

"Only if you need it to be."

From his spot on the floor, Berlin looked from you to Bob to you. To Bob again.

"He's a giant."

Bob exchanged a look with you, then looked back to Berlin. "Go on."

"That's all I've got, you think I asked for his ID? Why don't you track him the same way you tracked us?"

"This *is* how I tracked you. Tell me more before this gets ugly."

"Bald. White. Thick brown beard, even taller than me. Tattoo of a heart under his left eye."

"Fuck," Bob said under his breath. For a moment, there was silence—nothing but the ocean, still there. "Where'd you meet?"

"Made the pass on the red line last night, I think, you know the timeline's a little hazy. We didn't say shit to each other. That's all I know, I swear."

Bob nodded, satisfied. Then, he straightened his cuffs and made his way down the narrow aisle of the RV. He glanced at you: "I'll be in touch."

He left.

Berlin whistled. "Feels like it took a few times to get that one right, huh?"

"You're telling me."

"My ears are ringing."

"I feel like I've been below deck on a boat for about 3,000 years."

"Yeah," said Berlin. "Yeah, no shit. I know exactly what you mean."

You lapsed into silence again as if waiting for something. You half expected Bob to come back. You could hear a gun firing in your memory, faint, as though a brick wall had been built between you and that reality.

"I think this timeline's pretty safe," Berlin said, echoing the thought. "Not confident my customer's going to be too happy with me, but I think Bob's the bigger threat."

"Did you really sell all the time tabs?"

Berlin smiled. "Fuck no. But most of it."

"How did you know?"

"You told me. Yesterday. Have you not done that yet? Is that tomorrow?"

Fuck remembering. "Definitely tomorrow. Berlin, I'm glad it's gone. This has been crazy. And not good crazy."

"I think if we learn to take better control of it..."

"Stop. Maybe. We are not talking about this right now."

Berlin's expression turned grim. "Eventually, we won't have a choice."

"Let me just come down and chill and get away from the past for a minute. Ok?"

"You still have that page of tabs I gave you?"

You reached into your pocket, having almost forgotten them.

"Hold on to that," Berlin said. "I think you'll need it."

―――――

This is the conclusion of the ECHO3 timeline of volume 1.

*TURN to page 1 to begin again*

## 55

You scrambled out. This was all wrong. You felt sick.

Then, the sound of the gunshot struck through several realities; your consciousness bled across the severed boundary. It didn't feel like you were running, it felt like you were flying, no, suspended—

The air shimmered late afternoon.

You turned to look at the RV.

There was Bob, dragging Berlin out of it, Berlin's torso bloody and his head hung limp.

*No.*

*Fuck.*

*How?*

You wanted to go to him. Fix this. Jump backwards— would the boundary bend that far? Past death? What if you had reached a place from which things could not be fixed? It's not like you were a chemist or theoretical physicist, you didn't know how this shit worked. Where were the worlds this drug created in relation to reality? And where did they go?

Staying here was dangerous. A mistake, a corruption. Staying threatened permanence. Now was the time to act, undo. Out at the edges, like the storm clouds coming in. Staying here was a place you couldn't come back from. And there was that piece of paper in your pocket, calling your name.

*To* RUN *towards Berlin and Bob, turn to page* 139

*To take one of the time tabs in your pocket, go to page* 142

## 56

### VIOLENT DELIGHTS

You grabbed a beer bottle out of last night's six pack, still sitting out on your little foldout kitchenette. Bob's attention was on Berlin, all menacing hunched shoulders. You wound up, took aim, and struck Bob on the side of the head as if you were wielding a baseball bat. The bottle shattered as it made contact, and blood spurted from Bob's skull as he collapsed.

You and Berlin stared at Bob's crumpled body for a long beat.

"Shit," said Berlin.

You looked at the bottle in your hand, still raised. You dropped it. "What do we do now?"

Berlin rose to his full height, stepped forward, and prodded Bob with his foot. "Help me move him outside. Then, we get out of here."

You bent to take Bob under his arms, Berlin grabbed his feet. Together you lifted him and shuffled through the hall of the RV, down the stairs, out the door, and onto the pavement of the parking lot. Berlin sank down onto the

RV's front bumper ran his hand through his hair, and looked to you.

"We best start running," said Berlin.

"Lin..."

"Whatever you're going to say, you've already said. Just... think of me."

On the ground, Bob groaned.

"Come on," he said, "let's get going."

Berlin turned, headed back inside. You hesitated.

IF YOU REGRET YOUR ACTIONS, *turn to page 144*

*If you want to high tail it out of here, turn to page 148*

## 57

# THE NOBODY DOCTRINE

You had to stay, you could not leave him, even as the edges of your vision blurred as other realities seeped in. Whoever Bob Smith was and wherever he came from, he had the upper hand. There was only you, no one, here to protect Berlin, also no one. Nobodies looked out for each other, as there was no one else to do it. This was your lot in life. This was the future.

Bob waved his knife at you with the air of a casual gesture. "Not bad," he said, "not bad."

"I'm not doing this to impress you," you said.

Bob smirked, all unsettling confidence. He raised his chin and with an air of superiority asked: "Do you know where Berlin got that gun?"

You turned to Berlin. Berlin wouldn't look at you.

"Why don't you ask him?" Bob goaded. "Mr. Halifax, where'd you get that gun?"

"Shut up!" Berlin spat.

"And for what? Come on now, fight like a man. That was your intention, wasn't it? See if you can stop me."

Berlin shoved you aside. The shot rang out. And Bob was gone.

Just that: gone. Not dead: vanished.

"What the fuck?" Berlin said.

"That's what I was gonna ask you."

"I don't know," Berlin murmured, shaking his head. "I don't know."

"Where *did* you get that gun?"

"Work thing. Doesn't matter. We're safe now, aren't we?"

'Safe' seemed a dubious assumption. "Hmmm."

"Don't worry about it. Listen, I owe you one. Putting your life in the way like that..."

"It's nothing."

"Not to me."

"What do we do now?" you asked.

"I don't know. You still tripping?"

"Pretty hard, yeah."

"Me too. I'm gonna try to head this Bob thing off if I can. I only just made it back in time. I'm getting better at controlling the temporal boundary."

"Ok," you said, full of a sudden fondness. Frustrated as you were by the danger you found yourselves in, there was something so prototypically *Berlin* about it that you couldn't help but smile. His recklessness combined with his desire for control. The way you got swept along with it. That's why you'd chosen this life, after all. "You fix everything. I'm just gonna lie down."

Berlin laughed: relieved, perhaps, by the ease of your demeanor. "Yeah yeah. Just don't get lost in time while I'm gone."

And yet, that seemed like exactly what your body wanted to do. As the stress and paranoia brought on by Bob unwound, you felt yourself almost floating. Time spun around you, and all you wanted was to lay back and witness it; let the current take you away.

You tried to use what you knew of the drug to tune into your trip, to control it without grabbing on too tight. You conjured your desired moment in your mind's eye and focused.

You were there.

IN THE RED ARROW DINER? *Turn to page* 32
Or tripping in the camper? Turn to page 95

## 58

"...**W**hat sort of things?" asked Berlin.

"Whatever nefarious things it is you've assumed I'm doing," said Bob, "let me show them to you."

"Fuck you."

"Philosophy is not your strength, Mr. Halifax. It is your deftness and cunning."

"You think *I* have a corrupted moral center?" Berlin asked, which is when he pulled out the gun.

You're not sure what happened next. You had closed your eyed and ducked.

Then there were sirens. The red and blue lights coming in, staining everything. Mostly red. Red red red. That was when your trip slipped you away, pulled you out of that terrible moment.

You were on the subway. You were leaning on Berlin's shoulder.

"That's right. Stay here. Come over to this timeline, with me. We got this. Just sink up."

But the wail of the siren pierced your consciousness

like a drill. Outside they were loading Berlin into the ambulance. You were just hoping no one would question you, that they would leave you alone.

But it wasn't going to be that simple.

Bob reentered the van and came straight for you. He tried to put on a kind face, but you saw through it, almost sickened by the facade. That's how all grown-ups were, with that face. It disgusted you.

Maybe your disgust showed, because Bob's false kindness faded grey. "Tell me where to find the hotel," he said.

"I don't know."

"I can fix things for you," Bob said. "Berlin leaves the hospital all better. Your little girlfriend has a change of heart. You finally get an opportunity. But I'm gonna need a little more cooperation."

*To tell Bob what you know, turn to page 109*

*To refuse to cooperate, turn to page 152*

## 59

___

You couldn't just leave him. Not if this was real, even in some small way. There had to be a timeline where you didn't, where you stayed. Loyal to a fault. To your friend.

Time seemed to move slower. A part of you felt the current carrying you away upstream, to page 134, but another part of you, the part that longed for justice, anchored itself in the present and struggled forward.

Bob saw you coming as he laid Berlin's body down in an empty spot adjacent to the RV; Berlin's red blood smeared on the faded delineating lines. There was a storm coming in. The wind of it lifted your hair. The skies grew darker.

"It's not pretty," he said, straightening his cuffs (his wrists tattooed with spades). "But it comes with the territory."

"Take it back."

Bob arched a brow. Then he turned away from you and looked beyond the RV, to the storm. He stepped out of the way of Berlin's blood, seeping. He looked to you again. "Storm's coming in."

"I can see that."

"Yes. But do you know what it means?"

"I want my friend back!"

"And I want justice," Bob replied, aplomb. "Perhaps, in another life, these desires could find themselves more compatible."

"Shut up," you said, wanting to hurt him, scared to. You did not know where Berlin's gun had gone. "He didn't have anything to do with—he got mixed up in this. He wasn't going to kill you, he's not a killer. You didn't have to kill him."

"How do you know what he is and isn't? What he might become?" Bob reached into his pocket and withdrew a pack of Lucky Strikes and a matchbook. He stuck a cig in his mouth, struck the match along the back of the matchbook, then, with a flare, brought the lit match to the tip of the smoke and inhaled. It ignited with a warm orange glow as Bob breathed in, in. Smoke expelled from the sides of his mouth and he dropped the still-lit match onto Berlin's body.

"In my line of work," Bob said, "the lines between what needs to be done, what has to be done, what can be done, what should be done, and what *will* be done... well, were there ever any lines in the first place?" He paused to blow a smoke ring, let it expand, then blew a second smoke ring through it. "With some people, it's important to make a strong impression."

It started to rain.

"What happens now?" you asked.

Bob smiled. The cigarette smoke lingered around him, not dissipating, and began now to cloud his face. "I already told you." The orange tip glowed through the smoke as Bob took another drag and expelled another puff, the smoke now engulfing you. You went to step back, but found that you couldn't, as if your attention were a physical part of you upon which Bob had taken hold. "I'll see you in the future."

The rain fell heavier, and the smoke grew thicker, and somewhere, you thought you heard the sound of a train.

*T*URN *to page 68*

## 60

_____

This would be for the best.

You ducked behind a car and took the sheet of acid tabs in your pocket. There were a few tabs missing, which you didn't precisely remember, but something about it feels familiar, like, '*uh oh.*'

Which was fine. This was fine. Everything was going to be fine.

*Berlin is dead over there,* you thought.

Just take it. Take it, and fix it. That's how it worked. It was that simple.

You ripped off a tab—you know what? Fuck it. Two. And you took them.

You collapsed against the car and closed your eyes while they dissolved. Oh, shit, this was so, so bad. There was no way out of this. This was hopelessly fucked up, and you were going to be stuck in this trip forever. Literally. Your consciousness was stretching out, out, out.

Rolling down the street on your longboard, but the street was made of celluloid. Standing bored in the liquor store, staring at a leak in the ceiling. Not dripping yet. Not dripping yet. Not dripping yet. Not dripping yet... The stain looked a bit like Russia. *Not a winner, not a winner, not a winner*. Startling at the sound of a gunshot that wasn't really there.

Berlin coming home, Berlin telling you everything...

"Berlin, we can't," you said.

"What do you mean, we can't?"

*To stop this before it starts, turn to page 24*

## 61

## AN UNLIKELY ECHO

"We better get out of here," Berlin said, watching Bob. He took one step onto the first stair and turned to look at you. "You coming?"

You looked at Bob. He wore on his wrist what you understood to be a new-fangled watch, all black and shiny. Its screen was cracked. Did that just happen?

The acid was still playing with your mind and vision. Berlin swam before you, almost a mirage. The night seemed to have flattened into a watercolor painting; you could reach up and touch the moon—but you wouldn't. You were worried of what might happen if you did.

Time spun itself before you like a treadmill. You could almost hear it whir.

You could almost hear Bob saying, *I want to help you. I want to help. Help. Help.* like a broken record at the back of a cave.

"Hello?"

"Sorry," you said. "I'm still trippin, man."

Berlin nodded: that satisfied him. In response, you felt a sudden and involuntary lurch of hatred.

"Well come on. We can't hang around here forever, he's going to wake up."

As if to reinforce this, Bob groaned again and started pushing himself to his feet. Berlin gave him a good, sharp kick in the gut for good measure.

"I'm staying with him," you said, bending to touch his back. He slumped back to the ground.

"What?"

"Go. I'll give you that, you're my best fucking friend. But I can't take this anymore, Lin. I'm not getting any more tangled up in this. Go now, don't tell me where you're going. Hide. But stay away from me. Keep me out of this."

It was hard to see in the dark, but you felt Berlin's expression anyway. Shocked. Hurt. Confused.

"Do you even know what this guy *represents?*"

"Hey, I helped you, didn't I? I did the right thing! But I don't know what's going on anymore, Berlin, I'm seeing sideways and in circles, and you barely even gave me a 'heads up!' Maybe I don't want to get tangled up in something like this! Maybe I just want to lie low and find Violet!"

"Violet? Come on, Violet?! She's nobody! She's a kid!"

"Shut the fuck up, she's everything. I'll fuck you up, too!"

Berlin laughed. "You? Fuck *me* up?" He climbed a few more steps into the RV and caught the door before it swung shut. "See you on the other side," he said. The door closed.

The engine started. The RV drove away.

You were now homeless.

"You got one thing wrong, kid," was the first thing Bob said to the dark, a long time after Berlin drove away.

"What's that?" you asked.

"There's no backing out of this one. The only way out is through."

———

This is the conclusion of the ECHO4 timeline of volume 1.

To RETHINK *your choices in the RV, turn to page 95*
*To back all the way out, return to page 1*

## 62

---

"We use the heat register under the cupboard in the back room to stash important stuff," you said, hating yourself. But what choice did you have? It was almost as though all of this had happened before, already.

Bob went to take a look. You heard him jiggling with the register grate until it came free.

"There's nothing here," Bob said.

You felt a sudden rush of relief. And then, as if Berlin were gently nudging you, you were reminded of the small square of tabs currently folded in your front pocket.

You reached for them and tried to rip off a small piece blind. Just enough to change how this goes. Just enough.

"Did you hear me? I said there's nothing in here! Do you have any other bright ideas?"

TURN *to page* 151 *to take the time tab*

## 63

## COMMUNITY CHEST

"We better get out of here," Berlin said, watching Bob. He took one step onto the first stair and turned to look at you. "You coming?"

"Yeah," you said, forcing yourself to look away from the crumpled man. "Yeah, of course."

You both climbed in. Berlin dropped right into the driver's seat, hit the brake, and pressed the button to start the ignition. The engine stuttered, complaining, but turned over, faithful as ever. You buckled into the passenger seat, and the RV pulled out of the parking lot and into the night. Berlin watched Bob out of the rearview mirror.

"Stay down, motherfucker," he muttered. "Stay down."

The future was going. And going. You pulled out of the parking lot. The road rolled on.

You were still tripping. You were flashing through timelines, lingering, sliding back. It filled you with an invigorating dizziness. And if you wanted, you could lift out of it, hover above, a moment of quiet. That's how it felt in the passenger seat of the RV, driving out into the dark.

"How long's this stuff last, anyway?" you asked.

"Hours, I think. But fuck me, it could be days. It's hard to tell, you know?"

"Yeah."

"I think it depends on how far back you go, but I think *that* also depends on how much you take... like I said, I'm not sure."

"And Bob Smith?"

"He's some secret agent or something trying to control all this shit. He wants to kill me."

"Because you stole his shit?"

"That's the short version."

"Yeah, I feel like we've had this conversation before."

"Don't you even start."

"Not starting."

You had reached the on ramp to the highway. Berlin got on Southbound and passed go.

———

This is the conclusion of the ECHO5 timeline of volume 1.

*To rethink Bob's input, go to page 95*

## 64

## THE MIDDLE

Oh, the effect was almost immediate. And what a *relief* it was to feel, now that you knew what to expect. The walls almost melting, washing you out of the RV, out of the scene, out of time, away from Bob and Berlin and all your messy choices. You would make it right this time.

For a long swirl of suspended black you floated nowhere, outside time, safe. But you could feel your trip pushing you along, encouraging you to hurry out of nothing, to be something again. But you didn't *want* to be something again. You wanted to go back before this all happened, to...

*Violet?* Turn to page 34

    *Bob?* Turn to page 57

    *Before it all began?* Turn to page 24

## 65

_____

"**Y**ou can't seduce me with your corruption."

Bob picked up the bottle you considered hitting him with and shook it at you.

"You think I'm just gonna let you walk away?" He brought the bottle up to his shoulder as if to swing, then said, "Take this one, too."

You weren't sure who he was talking to—but then, two EMTs grabbed you under the arms and hoisted you into the air. They were taking you too. They were taking you into the ambulance. Bob was laughing.

You thrashed, but they were way ahead of you: there was a needle piercing your skin, and then there was nothing.

TURN _to page_ 68

## 66

———

"You mean, like, get back to the Royal Oaks?"

Berlin shook his head. "No. I'm too easy to track down, there. We've got to go on the run."

You were not wild about this, especially considering the gravitational pull your last morning with Violet seemed to have on you; its mass the equivalent of a black hole. You couldn't just leave her. But here Berlin was, steering you away—one of the many downsides to sharing a mobile home.

"Can't you just sell your supply and wash your hands of it?"

"'Wash my hands?'" Berlin laughed. "Buddy, I get it, and I'm trying. But I don't think you're appreciating the magnitude of what's going on here." Berlin crossed the RV to his room and returned with a battered black backpack. The left strap held on by a thread and he'd drawn an encircled anarchy 'A' on the front pocket in silver sharpie. He unzipped the main compartment and showed you: two thick reams of the 4D-LSD. "I don't *want* to have to wash my hands. If we can start over with new names, we're set for life. Forget this fucking RV in this fucking hick hole town. We're gonna change the *world.*"

You gulped.

*IF YOU DISTRUST BERLIN, turn to page 156*

*To help Berlin, continue reading on the next page.*

## 67

---

What else could you do? He was your best friend.

"We'll go South while you ride out your trip, and we hole up in a motel until I get this figured out. In the meantime, if you see me in the past, tell me to be more careful."

It took a moment for you to wrap your mind around this concept. The time tab pulled at you with its long, strong fingers, a riptide into your memory of yesterday.

"Don't worry about this," said Berlin. "Trust me. I got you."

You collapsed backwards onto your sofabed.

To REMEMBER, *turn to page 158*

## 68

"Berlin... what are we talking about here? Are we risking our lives? Are you serious?"

Berlin yanked the backpack away and zipped it shut. "Of course I'm serious. Are *you* kidding?"

"No, I..."

"This is the cause. This is the *future*. This is the opportunity I've been waiting for my whole life."

"What are you gonna do, go back and buy Bitcoin?"

"Shut the fuck up."

"Sorry, Lin, this isn't exactly easy to wrap my mind around! Then what's the plan?"

"Fuck, I don't know. I... there's something I haven't been telling you."

"What?"

"When I got it... when I first did this deal, I mean, I... I tried some, obviously. Maybe too much. And I... well, you know me. When I get in over my head, I start swimming. But there's a world out there... powerful people. And they want what I have. So I say we keep it from them, and use it for ourselves in the meantime. There's got to be a way to do it, otherwise they wouldn't want to keep it from us so bad. You've seen how powerful this shit is, and you've only had a taste. What do you think?"

TO FOLLOW BERLIN, *turn to page 155*

*To sink up and stop this before it begins, turn to page 24*

## 69

---

"**K**id. Hey, kid. You there?"

You kept your eyes closed, hands buried in your hair. You were still in the RV, you knew it. You hadn't moved. Behind your eyes, your head pounded, eyelids red as if pierced by too-bright light. You hadn't moved, but time had moved around you. You were some-when else.

You pressed the palms of your hands into your eyes, pressure on the pain.

Berlin had led you wrong before. You had to admit that. Sneaking out the back doors of clubs and down alleys to avoid this ne'er-do-well or that. Throwing a 3am parade in New Orleans. And you could have done without the proclivity for coke (Super and otherwise). But this?

You looked up.

You were used to the blooming textures on the walls, the floor, the ceiling. You focused on the remarkable.

Before you was a man in dark glasses, a dark suit, white shirt, and a black hat. He carried in his right hand a black briefcase with a silver combination lock. And on his wrists, like cuff links, peeked out a pair of identical tattoos: spades.

The man sank to one knee and put his hand on your shoulder. You could see yourself reflected in his glasses. You could feel him looking at you.

"You're gonna get out of this," he said in a strong, steady voice. "And you're going to do it without hurting anybody."

The pain moved to your temples. The neurons were trying to burst right out of your brain. "What the Hell is going on?"

"You've taken a dosage of a drug known as Delta Tango Hotel. Your consciousness is expanding beyond the boundaries of the fourth dimension. Your future self is under supervision as we speak, and I've come back to help you."

"Who are you?"

"I told you." He released your shoulder to dip into his front suit pocket, his other arm resting on his bent knee. He pulled out a small scrap of paper — a business card — and handed it to you.

The business card read:

### BOB SMITH
Balance Management Agent
*Central Infrastructure Agency*

"The most important thing is staying calm," Bob said. "We don't want to alarm anyone. Let time slip by. Flow. Don't arrest it."

TO LET TIME SLIP BY, *turn to page* 162

*To arrest it, turn to page* 166

# 70

---

You tore off a whole column of perforated tabs and rested them on your tongue. You braced yourself. You weren't sure how a whole lot of the acid would hit you, but since you haven't exactly felt oriented to the past and future during your trip so far, you're hoping the side effects will be negligible.

*Save Berlin* was your anchor. *Help Berlin.*

TO REMEMBER THE HOSPITAL, *turn to page 13*

## 71

———

L et it slip by? You closed your eyes. Nothing could
be easier. Your memories were more than memories, a rush and wail of sound and color, like a dream. In
an instant, Bob Smith was swept away downstream, and
you in another current.

You were back in the diner. It was raining inside.
The water was up to your ankles again, sloshing
around. Violet hadn't seemed to notice. She was looking
at you.

"You seem nervous today," she said. "Something's
wrong."

*The ring is gone,* you were thinking, slipping seam-
lessly back into place as if you'd never left this moment.
*The ring is gone. I have to find it. How was it lost? Did I
take it—meaning, another version of me?*

And somehow this all felt familiar, like you'd lived it
before.

"Violet..." you said. "Something very strange is
going on."

You looked down at your hands like they had something to tell you. If they did, they didn't say.

Then, you saw the man. Bob Smith. He was sitting at the end of the bar, getting rained on. The rain dripped off his hat. He was watching you out of the corner of his eye. When he saw you see him, he smiled—just a quirk of his mouth.

The waitress came up to take your order.

"Two eggs over easy with wheat toast, a side of bacon, hold the home fries, sub hash browns."

The waitress took it all down dutifully and turned to you.

You were still looking at Bob Smith, so much so that Violet turned around to look at him, too. Even the waitress risked a glance after a moment, only to look back at you with her lips pursed, eyes veiling worry.

"Stay calm, kid," mouthed Bob Smith.

"Do you know that guy?" asked Violet.

"I... I feel like I've seen him somewhere. Like in a dream. Or another life."

Violet laughed. "Yeah, ok, something's definitely wrong. I mean, you can be spacey but... 'seen him in another life?' Who says that?"

"Your breakfast, dear?"

*The ring was gone.* Don't panic, but how aren't you supposed to panic if the ring is gone?

"It was Berlin," said Bob. "Remember?" Now Bob was sitting across from you instead of Violet. Violet was gone. The waitress was gone.

*"Where's Violet?"*

"She's safe, in the future, far from this collapsing timeline here. I'm sorry to tell you that your botched proposal is her reality."

"And *this?*" How could this be reality?

"It isn't reality," said Bob as if reading your mind. "It's a pocket just outside reality. I've chosen to meet you here to mitigate harm. Once the harmony here reaches a certain threshold of dissonance—which, by the looks of it, is very very soon—it'll simply pinch off. Like a bubble."

It was hard to wrap your head around this, here in the restaurant where it was raining. "And us?"

"Shadows of us. The dead skin of the conscious. We left our real selves back in the future. Is this making any sense?"

Your head was starting to hurt again. "A modicum."

"Adequate enough. Colloquially, it's known as 'sinking up.' While in this in-between state, it is possible to make—as far as we've discovered, minor changes to the timeline. This is where your friend Berlin comes in."

"Whatever he did, I'm not part of it. I don't know about it. He keeps me out of his business dealings."

"Your friend Berlin is a rotten dealer, little rabbit. He dealt you in. And he cheats."

"Cheats?"

Suddenly, Bob had your blue velvet ring box between the thumb and index finger of his left hand. You could see his cuff link tattoo—a club. "He went off and pawned it," Bob Smith said.

Again, your thoughts moved slower, waterlogged. "He what?"

"You heard me. We believe he used it to purchase a firearm."

*"My great grandmother's engagement ring?"*

"The very same. Your friend Berlin is a thief, little rabbit, thinking of himself before anyone. He has no regard for personal property. He stole from me, and now he stole from you."

It couldn't be true...

"But it is true," said Bob Smith. "Now, before this whole place collapses, how about you tell me where to find him?"

To TELL Bob what you know, turn to page 169

To keep Berlin's secrets, turn to page 172

## 72

_____

With car crash precision, as you halted your thoughts, you were thrown upward into the RV with Berlin. Only you weren't in the RV anymore, you were on the subway.

"Who the _Hell_ is Bob Smith?!"

"What? Did he find you?"

Oh, the train...

The advertisements looked the strangest, dancing and flashing. Fazing through each other in an illustrated history of airtime, rewound. It was easier to look at it than the other people. They weren't worms, the way Vonnegut had seen them. They were stacked on top of each other translucent, their lives shining right through their faces. Were they looking at you? Could they tell you were looking at them?

A light at the end of the car was blinking. Berlin asked for you again, but his voice was a distant echo under the sounds of the train, the wailing of the tunnel. And where you should have been able to feel the gentle rock of the train, the power of its speed, you felt nothing —you felt more as though you were suspended, midair, over a still pond with a full moon reflected in it.

And then you saw the man in the dark sunglasses, your own confused face reflected in the lenses.

"I *said*," he said through a gritted smile: "*relax.*"

"That's never as easy as people make it sound," you said, closing your eyes against the headache's return.

"Did he find you? *Where are you?!*"

Berlin again. He was shaking you by your shoulders.

"Enough, enough, I'm here," you replied, slouching away from him. "He found me. We're in the RV together. Who is he?"

"One of the many people who are *really* not happy with me. How did he find you?"

"Not sure. He... he says that he knows my future self."

"He could be lying. Don't trust a thing he says."

"What am I supposed to do? How did I get out of it, and get here?"

"Well, as long as you're here with me, you *do* get out of it."

"What, is there a possibility that I like, disappear?"

"I'm not really sure, I've only ever seen it from my perspective! You gotta have some sympathy here, with you all slumped over me and babbling like an idiot."

"*Sorry*, I've been *drugged!*"

"*Shh, shh!*" Berlin smiled around at the other people on the train. "Just having a bit of a breakdown. They're fine."

You hug yourself, already picturing the RV in your

head. Had that happened, earlier today? Had you met a stranger? Now that you've met him, you can't *not* remember it, but you're sure that's not what happened the first time around.

"You're trying to piece it together. I can hear you thinking. You can't do that. You have to relax. Remember too hard and you'll get all tangled up. Lose thread of all of it. Just relax into the trip. Follow where the path leads you. But do not, under any circumstances, tell Bob Smith where I am or where we're going."

TO TELL *Bob what you know, turn to page* 170

*To keep Berlin's secrets, turn to page* 173

## 73

---

"We live in an RV by the shore," you said.
"Where exactly?"
You told him.

"I don't know what's going on. I'm more of the tag-along guy, I swear. If I knew what he was up to I'd tell you. He just wants to get a motel. Hide out. He has lots of connections in the city, cause of the club scene."

You could tell Bob was not satisfied with your answer. The water was coming in.

"Find out more," he said. "I'll see you in the future." And then the wave burst through the door and swallowed you.

TO SINK UP, *turn to page 175*

# 74

---

"We live in an RV by the shore, but... now we're on a train going into the city..." you said, aware that you were saying it in both places, mumbling so Berlin couldn't hear.

"That's fine. I'll head you off before then. When did he leave to meet his connect?"

As you found your ground in the past, you sat up straighter, said it louder: "I don't know. I'm all fucked up. He left early afternoon, after this, and hasn't come back."

Bob's lips could not restrain something of a snarl before pressing together in a thin line. Then, he served you a somewhat forced grin and clapped you on your shoulders. "Excellent. Excellent. I knew there was something in you that would cooperate." He stood. "To business, then. Thank you for your help, it will be... remembered."

"That's it?" you asked. It was still raining in the diner, thought lighter than before, and without the flooding.

"You're not gonna... I don't know, explain what's going on?"

"Haven't I already? You've been so helpful, I only assumed..." The diner bloomed around him. "I suppose the memory lags a bit when you're green. Consider: when you think of me, you may remember more than what you've yet seen yourself."

OK. "What?"

"Your shadows." Bob stood up. He'd had his briefcase with him in the booth, he now held it by his side. "Don't worry too hard, little rabbit. When it doubt, go straight through."

*T*URN *to page* 177

# 75

---

"You think I'm just gonna betray my friend like that?"

"Why not? He betrayed you."

"According to some fascist in a suit that stalked me to a fucking diner. I don't know shit about you! And I don't talk to fucking cops!"

Bob shook his head. "I am not a cop."

"Well, figure something else out while you work the beat, cause I got this on my own. You're not getting *shit* from me."

Bob was unmoved. You even saw the shadow of a smile. "We'll see about that," he said.

You left the booth. You had to find Violet. You had to find the engagement ring and fix this whole mess. Oh, the hexagon rain. You opened the door to leave the diner and were hit by a tsunami so powerful it snapped your neck.

To sink up, *turn to page 68*

## 76

"Screw you," you told Bob with a snarl.

"Tut tut. That's not very professional."

"*Screw you!*"

"Just calm down! Time trips can be overwhelming. I can see your head splitting from future feedback. Tune it out. We don't want you to lose your mind, do we?"

The future roared like radio static. Berlin: worried, worried. Running, shedding off the past like snakeskin. Whoever this was: after him. Come on, 'Bob Smith?' He was a facade, he was the face of power.

"You represent everything I despise," you spat. "Leave me and my friends alone."

Bob slapped you.

For a moment, the blooming RV walls seemed to quiet. Everything seemed to quiet. You could feel the slap echoing through your other selves, stretched across the fourth dimension.

"I know more. I know better. I have been keeping the

timelines in balance for longer than you've been alive. I won't have gutter rats like you telling me I'm scum."

Your face stung.

You rode the shockwave straight into the future.

*To sink up, turn to page 181*

## 77

---

The little patterns pulsing on everything around you seemed to take a sterner shape, scolding you. Oh, because of you, there was danger. You'd betrayed yourself just then. You'd got lost down a rabbit hole and trusted a trickster: you could see the shapes of your fate unfolding like an origami rose. Oh, Berlin would be cross with you. How he'd trusted you, your friend.

You jerked up on your sofabed (now bed) in the RV. You scrambled around for your phone, peeked out the window. Where were you? *When* were you? There was something nagging at your memory—like something larger than yourself was begging you to remember.

You were in the trailer park a few hours from where you started yesterday. Today? Berlin was not there.

All was quiet. You searched around for his backpack, his things—nothing. It was night. And Berlin wasn't there. You checked his usual hiding spots (even the heating grate behind his bed). Neither was the tango hotel. All this moved through your mind very slowly, like a lecture you'd heard before but hadn't listened to.

You scrambled around your for your phone to find the date.

But your phone was gone, too.

"What the fuck," you said, throwing your blankets off the bed, then scrambled around checking all the places it usually was, not on the counter

Did you... did you do something to cause Berlin's absence? When did he stash this? How did he disappear? Where were *you,* passed out on a couch in the past? Was he okay? Did you doom him?

Something was wrong. You were still tripping, and the future felt black. Guilt ate away at your stomach. What had you done? And then, the missing ring—what had *Berlin* done? Everything seemed to lead back there, like a bathtub drain, whirlpool spinning. The scene threatened to overtake you, sweep you away again: panic and desperation.

You rifled through the stack of acid.

TURN *to page* 185

# 78

---

"**W**ait—!"

But the timeline popped.

You jerked up on your sofabed (now sofa) in the RV. You scrambled around for your phone, peeked out the window. Where were you? *When* were you? There was something nagging at your memory—like something larger than yourself was begging you to remember.

You were in the trailer park. Today? Yesterday? Berlin was not there. Your phone was nowhere to be found, which concerned you, but you had rather enough to deal with to waste too much thought on something misplaced.

All was quiet. You searched around for Berlin's backpack, his things—nothing. You took stock of what you knew: it was night. It was night, and Berlin wasn't there. Neither was the LSD. All this moved through your mind very slowly, like a lecture you'd heard before but hadn't listened to.

It occurred to you, there was one place—the panic

box, as you called it. A loose grate in the corner of Berlin's bedroom where he stashed some loose cash and—

And nothing. The panic box was empty. In fact, Berlin's room was eerily clean, untouched, unlived in.

Did you... did you do something to cause Berlin's absence? Where had he gone? Where and when were *you,* passed out on a couch in the past? Was he okay? Did this have something to do with the man from the diner — had you doomed him?

Something was definitely wrong. You were still tripping, and the future felt black. Guilt ate away at your stomach. What had you done? And then, the missing ring —what had *Berlin* done? Everything seemed to lead back there, like a bathtub drain, whirlpool spinning. The scene threatened to overtake you, sweep you away again: your panic and desperation at the empty ring box bubbling through you.

You hardened yourself to it, you could not allow yourself to lose control. Wasn't that exactly what Berlin had warned you about? And yet here you were, the time tab buffeting you about like a bird in a hurricane.

What had the man at the diner said? 'The only way out was through?' You reached into your pocket and withdrew the sheet of time tabs Berlin had given you. How were you supposed to go straight though an experience that was inherently disorienting? How do you master it? Take more?

To take a tab, *turn to page 188*

To take nothing, *turn to page 185*

## 79

You woke in the passenger seat of the RV, flying down the highway while Berlin stood on the accelerator.

"Good. You're up. How are you feeling?"

You looked around. The world looked a bit less trippy, though still distorted, and there was an itch in your brain like a memory you'd forgotten.

"Bob found us," Berlin continued, unmoved by your silence. "No idea how he did it. This is *nuts*."

"How'd we end up here?"

"Took another tab. My tolerance is through the roof, only knocked me back a few hours. But that was enough to head Bob off and hit the highway. But it's only a matter of time before he catches up. He's always a step ahead, that sonovabitch."

"He can't catch us if there's nothing to catch. Slow down, Lin, before we're both splats on the pavement."

Berlin refused to slow.

"I need you to do something for me."

"'Something?' Are you serious?"

"Dead serious. I need you to fix this."

"Oh, great, let me get right on that!"

"I'm serious. Take another tab, go back to this afternoon, tell me not to go. Stop me from going. I'd do it myself, but like I said. I fucked up my tolerance, I need to dry out."

"Lin, I am still actively tripping. You want me to take more?"

"Listen, if you're high enough to close your eyes and sink up wherever you please, do it! If you're not, please, take another dose. For me..."

You were relaxed. You could sink up, if you wanted to. But what did you want to remember?

To remember the diner, *turn to page* 34

To remember Bob, *turn to page* 99

*To stop yourself from taking the drug when it's first offered, turn to page* 24

## 80

# THE FUTURE

You were flying down the highway in the RV, which shook under the duress of Berlin standing on the accelerator. You were buckled in to the passenger seat.

"Good. You're up. How you feeling?"

You looked around. The world looked a bit less trippy, though still distorted, almost itching.

"Bob found us," Berlin continued, unmoved by your silence. "No idea how. This is *nuts.*"

"How'd we get here?"

"Took another tab. The more often you take it, the less far back you go. I was aiming for this afternoon and ended up about an hour ago. It's like I built up some sort of time tolerance."

"Jesus, Lin, how many holes are you gonna rip in the space-time continuum?"

"I *think* the leaks damn themselves," Berlin said, more to himself than you. "I think it's a self-balancing entity. So whatever the Hell they think they're doing, it's fruitless as fuck all." He cackled, throwing his head back and everything. "Fuck 'em!"

"Slow down, will you? Forget Bob, you're gonna get us killed."

"'Forget Bob?' Buddy, if dying in a car accident is your biggest concern right now, I don't know what to tell you."

"You're tripping balls!"

Berlin eased up on the gas pedal a little.

"*We* are tripping balls," he said, which made you laugh a little.

"What did you want to do earlier today?"

"Stop myself from doing what I did," said Berlin. "But it's too late. It's whatever."

"What did you do?"

Berlin didn't answer.

"If you stole the drugs, I don't care. Obviously the military didn't want this getting out."

"Yeah," said Berlin. "Yeah, exactly."

"How did you do it?"

"I don't regret stealing it," said Berlin. "It's something else. Something with... consequences. A leak that might be too big to dam."

"What, did you kill somebody?"

Berlin didn't answer.

"Berlin, *are you serious?*"

"I didn't kill anybody."

"What, then?"

"I... I took a shitload of it. Went back about three months."

"Why?"

"Because Bob Smith, that's why."

Speak of the devil, and Bob Smith was on your tail.

You weren't sure how it happened. Had he found you in these handful of minutes when Berlin stopped burning gas? It was so certainly him—a black car with a shining silver grille, round headlights, and a black license plate that read "BOBSMITH" in white letters.

"Shit," Berlin said. "Shit, shit, shit shit."

"What do we do?"

"You need to go back," Berlin said. "There's gotta be another way out of this."

"Listen, if you're turning your head into Swiss cheese..."

"I'm not, damn it! I—if I could do it myself, I would. But I can't. I've fucked up things enough already. I'm not asking for much. I—I just want you to try telling me not to go. When I go to leave today. Just... just tell me not to go."

"What, and kill us?"

"And kill this *timeline!* I'm not exactly thrilled with the consciousness I'm perceiving right now, are you? Just one last time, go back, and this whole bloated universe will pinch right off and go to Heaven!"

Bob was gaining.

"Okay," you said. "I'll try."

Berlin reached into his pocket and pulled from it a folded sheet of acid tabs. None of the tabs were missing, unless whole columns had been torn away.

"Keep those on you, just in case," Berlin said. "I've got plenty."

But it just felt so wonderful, coming down, getting out...

"Well? Are you gonna take it, or not?"

You couldn't refuse Berlin.

To take the time tab, *turn to page 190*

*To end this all before it begins, turn to page 24*

# 81

## THE HUNT

Stay out of it, just stay out of it. Stay here, removed, in the quiet. But of course, you were antsy. Worried. You needed to act.

You tried texting Violet. Sure, she rejected you this morning, but that was a flooded diner and several universes ago. Anything could change in an afternoon, especially while the timeline was in flux. Right?

No answer.

You waited around for a while, wondering. You studied the delta tango hotel, which, aside from being a fourth dimension psychedelic hallucinogen, seemed unremarkable. Just paper, really. Paper stained with chemistry. But something gnawed at you, echoing in the back of your mind—it was like you could hear Violet crying for help, singing out to you as if from the shower. Violet? Violet?

There was also the issue of Bob Smith. Where had he gone? Hadn't he said that he owed you something, for helping him? Was this payback: leaving you alone in a dead silent future?

Because it wouldn't stop bothering you, you opened the internet on your phone and searched for Violet's name. It's not an uncommon name, and she shared it with a Sherlock Holmes character. But when you filtered the results by news, then by location, you found what you were looking for. Your stomach was a black pit of dread.

FOUL PLAY SUSPECTED IN HUNTER DISAP-PEARANCE

Violet Hunter, 23, student at Royal Oaks University, disappeared under mysterious circumstances on Friday, October 13, 2035. While the Royal Oaks police department deny evidence of foul play, the Greater Oaks police chief feels the case worthy of investigation.

Violet Hunter was last seen leaving her dormitory around 5:00 on October 13th. Violet is an exemplary student—

You threw your phone aside.

*"Fuck!"*

You had to go back. You *had* to go back. What had happened? Was Bob involved? There had to be a way to fix this...

Before you were even conscious of your decision, you had drawn a sheet of acid tabs from the pile and ripped off a tiny perforated square. You balanced it on the tip of your index finger and examined the cartoon rabbit's swirling eyes, alive and moving. You placed the tab on your tongue.

What did you want to remember?

To GO TO THE DINER, *turn to page* 34

*To confront Bob Smith, turn to page* 99

*To stop yourself from taking the drug when it's first offered, turn to page* 24

## 82

---

Yes, you would take more. You would revisit the past, try again. That would be the right thing.

You couldn't leave him. And the ring—it had to be somewhere. There had to be some way to recover it. All you had to do was go back.

Did fragments of other timelines still exist? Could they be re-done, rewritten, or were they loose threads adding to the chaos? What if, in taking this new dose, you were jumping into shadow? What if the adventure looped back and always ended here?

But what if it didn't?

And what about the ring? It all seemed to center around its disappearance, the rip in time upon which all this chaos rent. Had you—had some version of you snuck into your past and stolen the ring for some reason or other: to stop your proposal? To, perhaps, favor someone else? Something twisted in your gut at that prospect, almost pleasure. A thrill of the forbidden, of foreboding, that your future self might look out for yourself like that. What if Bob had lied?

Who are you to understand how it works, really? All you knew was that it was swallowing you, the past, the future, these hallucinations. Your memory throbbed in the back of your brain, a physical ache, tangible panic. It was your duty to fix this, to try. Your body was telling you so.

Wasn't it?

Now was the time to close your eyes, sink back a moment, decide differently. But how much of the time tab to take?

To TAKE A FULL TAB, *turn to page* 34
    *To take half a tab, turn to page* 57
    *To bite off the tiniest corner, turn to page* 158

## 83

———

Such a fuzzy feeling... pleasant, euphoric, at peace. The world was rushing by you in a whirl of color and light, color and light, with a splash of darkness. There was somewhere you were going, but you couldn't remember where, but the scenery was so pleasant that you did not mind anyway.

The patterns! How bizarre and intricate they were, alive! The Earth was alive! And it moved in patterns, the exact same patterns, every time, even if you went back and rearranged one thing, the rest would fall in line, fall in line, until it was all congruent again, congruent again.

There was the RV, there was the diner, there was the missing ring, there was Violet, there was Bob, there was Berlin Berlin Berlin, and the time travel drug in his backpack... how central it felt, now, a fulcrum, before and after, life, life.

You landed in a memory, remembering. What did you want to remember?

·  ·  ·

To REMEMBER THE DINER, *turn to page* 34

To remember Bob Smith, *turn to page* 57

To break Berlin out of the hospital, *turn to page* 161

To stop yourself from taking the drug when it's first offered, *turn to page* 24

## 84

You sipped. There was something so calming and centering about a sip of Supercoke. Sure, it was probably thanks to the decades of internalized advertising that convinced you to associate it with happiness and home, but it *worked* goddamnit, like a dream.

The walls started pulsing with the beat of the music. You bobbed your head along, tapping your hand to the rhythm against the bar. Berlin smiled at you, all aglow in nightclub neon. Trinity leaned forward on her elbow and put her chin in her palm.

"So, are you all secrets? Or..."

"Trinity, Trinity," said Berlin. "Curiosity killed the cat, you know."

"That's why we have nine lives."

"Shut up. I'm not telling you."

"Come on!"

Berlin held up his hands, mock-innocent. "No, it's true. We are staying out of it. All we gotta do now is close the loop. That was my mistake the first time."

"If ever you want to start making sense, I'll be over here, *working.*" She drew a tear down her cheek with her index finger and sauntered off to the other end of the bar, where patrons were waiting.

The walls pulsed with greater energy, undulating with a slither as the beat went *thunthunthunthununthunthunthun.* And now, the scene stretched, slower and wider, like it took longer to move through each moment, and the past and future vignette lingered in the air.

Oh shit. Oh shit, oh shit, oh shit. It was in the Supercoke, you fucking idiot. You'd been drugged.

"Lin... you... shithead... idiot... we were supposed to stop it..."

You took in your surroundings. The club, right. The... the subway car you took to get here. Further: the RV. Oh, maybe....

You shook it off. This couldn't be happening. You were back in the *Delta Variant,* gripping the bar with white knuckles as if that would keep you in reality. You had drunk half of your fucking Supercoke. Jesus Christ. It just slipped by.

"You drugged me," you said. "You fucking idiot, I'm trying to save your life!"

There was Trinity at the other end of the bar, head tilted toward you, half-listening. Her eyes narrowed, suspicious and concerned. "What?"

"He slipped some fucking acid into my fucking drink! I'm fucking tripping!"

You were back in the RV, alone. Someone was knocking on the door.

"Don't fight it, don't fight it, that just makes it worse,"

Berlin was saying, his hand on your shoulder in the club. "We just have to close the loop, hear me? Or time collapses, and we'll all end up—"

"Don't touch me!"

"I'm sorry!" Berlin let go. "I didn't know what to do, there isn't any other way! I need you in on this, you have to understand! My fucking life is at stake at this point. You gotta get in on this interdimensional chess!"

Fury. "We gotta get *out!*"

Trinity looked disgusted. "Berlin, boundaries!"

"Stay out of this, Trin, if you know what's good for you."

She arched an eyebrow, crossed her arms, and came close again. "Excuse me?"

"Did I stutter?"

Trinity reached across the bar and gave Berlin a sharp shove in the chest.

"Hey!"

TO TRUST BERLIN, *turn to page 202*

*To leave the bar with Trinity, continue reading on the next page.*

## 85

You wanted to shove him too. The room was spinning, the fluorescent silver subway of the recent past a vignette at the edges of your vision. Berlin was ready to fight back. You were ready to fall.

"Trinity," you said, clinging to the current moment. "Trinity! Leave it!" You reached across the bar and pulled her back by the scruff of her shirt. She swore at you.

"That's not cool," Trinity said, shaking you off. "At my bar? Come on, man. Not fucking cool."

Berlin was not having it. "'*Your*' bar? This is *my* bar. Don't go mouthing off about shit you don't understand. 'Your' bar. *Please.*"

It was hard to keep your head here. Your consciousness stretched its neck out the window as far as it could, trying to count the stars. The gas station. The diner. A girlfriend. Home.

You could smell home: your mother's cooking, the

carpet of your childhood bedroom. The bar before you shimmered like water disturbed by stones, rings echoing out, out, and in their wake was the highway, your college classrooms, the kitchen table. You went to hide under the kitchen table, far away from this, and were met with Trinity taking hold of your arm.

"Come on," she said, "let's get out of here."

"Come *on,*" Berlin said, "you gotta be kidding—"

"Stay the fuck away from us," Trinity said, all tough, and if you'd been paying attention you'd have seen the pocket knife she held in Berlin's face. You focused, you sank back into the moment, you saw it again: a short, blunt knife with a black blade and stickers on the handle. Trinity's tattoos bloomed, moving. Berlin backed off.

Trinity took your hand and pulled you through the teeming mass of concert-goers. The bodies seemed to leave shadows of themselves behind as they danced like a long exposure photo. You were hyperaware of the histories of each dancer, as if those trains of light and color extended beyond the bar, through town, along the winding paths that led them here all the way back to the moment of conception. It stretched forward, too, to graduations and weddings and early deaths at the hands of cancer or motorcycles. It was too, too much; it was better to see a crowd as an anonymous mass, and nothing more. Now it was all light, all light.

But Trinity had your hand, squeezing it, leading you, protecting you. And then you burst out into the open air: cool night, rustling trees, and infinite stars.

"You ok?" Trinity asked.

You swallowed and nodded. Trinity shimmered in dark.

"You can sleep it off at my place. I don't want you back in that camper van until you're sober. At the very least."

To go to Trinity's, *continue reading on the next page.*

## 86

Trinity took you back to her apartment in her little solarcar. There was barely enough room in it for the two of you.

In the past, in the RV, there was a knock at the door. Or was it the future? Somehow you had come unmoored and now it all blended together. Trinity's car drove through a stretch of road suspended above the multiverse, with all the potential pasts and futures reflected like blue light in the passenger window. Was that Berlin, dead, in your memory? Was that a man in a suit lying crumpled on the ground at sunset? Were these memories even real, or fantasies? They were water in your cupped hands.

"How do you feel?" Trinity asked as she flicked on her turn signal (left).

"Weird," you replied, head pounding. "It helps to hear you talk. It keeps me here."

"I'm gonna kill that fucking bastard."

That made you smile. "Don't do that."

"Why not? I knew he was a son of a bitch, but I never

thought he'd sink to drugging his best friend. I mean, what's even the point?"

"That's the question." How do you explain this to Trinity? How do you tell her what you know when what you know was fast becoming what you knew? "I'm afraid if I tell you my theory, you'll think I'm crazy."

"Well, you're tripping, my friend, so yeah, anything you say very well could be crazy. But why don't you tell me anyway?"

You smiled. "Thanks for watching over me," you said. "Don't get too freaked out if I, you know."

"Start crying? See God? Shit yourself?"

"Or all 3."

"Ha! Listen, I'm forgiving, but please don't shit yourself in my apartment."

"No promises."

Trinity gave you a light punch to the arm. "We're almost there. You've never seen my place, have you?"

You shook your head, more in an effort to shake off the sudden premonition than as answer. For there was Trinity, seen from the back as she walked up the steps and unlocked the door to her third floor apartment. Small, with exposed brick, an overflowing sink, two cats coming up to greet her...

You squeezed your eyes shut and pinched the bridge of your nose. If you could just be nowhere, instead of everywhere. You were sick of seeing.

"Woah. You still good?"

"Mmm."

Trinity clucked her tongue as she parked the car, chastising Berlin again, you were sure. You had no memory of getting out of the car. But suddenly there was the foreseen memory, standing behind Trinity at her front door. Jangle of keys. Two cats.

For a moment, the jangle of keys transported you elsewhere, even further—your own keychain, TAKE IT EASY, BUT TAKE IT! NEW ORLEANS, LA—but the force of the present kept pulling. You followed Trinity in.

"What did Berlin mean when he said his first mistake was he didn't 'close the loop?'" Her tone was casual, but you could sense she'd been planning this moment your entire ride in the car. Looking back, you could see it in her posture, her grip on the wheel, the way she glanced at you. It clicked together with such force you were moved to speak.

In the parked solarcar, still buckled: "It expands your perception of time. I'm seeing wide. The past and future. It's trippy as Hell."

"You shitting me?"

"I don't know. I don't know how it works, I just know that it's happening."

So dark in the car. Such a small, dim kitchen. Two cats.

*Click* as Trinity unbuckled. "I'm gonna have to think about this."

"It's fine if you think I'm crazy. Thanks for letting me crash."

"Of course."

The kitchen: "What did Berlin mean when he said his first mistake was he didn't 'close the loop?'"

The room spun with such force that you stumbled, and Trinity lowered you into a straight-backed kitchen chair. You put your head between your knees for a second, squeezed your knees against your temples.

Eyes shut, you said: "I don't know. I was trying to stop it. I don't know what he's trying to do."

"What can I do to help?"

"You're doing enough. I'm sorry to bother you like this." Your head was still between your knees, but the room was spinning less, at least. You slowly unwound upright, and as you did, your own body left a long exposure trail.

"Don't even. Want water? Supercoke?"

FOR WATER, *turn to page 204*

For Supercoke, *turn to page 208*

## 87

The high settled in familiar. Knowing it made you confident, moving through time like a wave.

"Trinity, relax, it's fine. He's right, we got a loop to close. I was joking. Just get me a water, okay?"

Trinity narrowed her eyes at you. "You sure?"

"Positive."

"Knew you'd come around," Berlin smiled.

"Shut up. You could have at least asked."

"If you haven't noticed, delta tango hotel doesn't exactly 'ask.'"

"Sometimes you are such a fucking prick."

"Thank you."

Trinity gave you your water with a begrudging little pout. "If you don't tell me what's going on I'm calling the cops."

Berlin looked affronted. "You wouldn't dare."

"Watch me."

Berlin shot you a significant look. "We're damning a leak."

"Oh, shut up, what's that supposed to mean?"

"We're plumbers now," you offered.

"Okay, Mario," Trinity rolled her eyes. "He roofied you so you can go be a plumber?"

"Yes," Berlin said, taking you by the arm. "Exactly. Let's go."

To LEAVE THE CLUB, *turn to page* 206

## 88

———

"I 'll have a water," you said. "Just gonna try to clear my head and sleep this off."

"Yeah, of course!" She tossed you a plastic bottle from the fridge. "I'll get you set up on the sofa. You just sit tight."

One of Trinity's cats—the black one with one eye—rubbed up against your leg and meowed at you. You meowed back.

"That's Alice," said Trinity, as she emerged from a doorway on one side of the kitchen with an armful of blankets. "The white one's Pip." She passed through the other doorway to her little living room and started draping them over her sofa, fluffing a pillow so it was just so. You couldn't find Pip. But for a moment there seemed to be two of Alice, purring as they rubbed their heads up against each other. The opposite Alice had her eye in the opposite place.

But when you went to scratch under the chin of the right-eyed Alice, she disappeared. The proper Alice bumped her head into the void where she wasn't, accepting the scratch. Her fur was so soft. You could feel her purr.

Your future was not far away. A parallel something tugged at your consciousness—the fizz of carbonation, blue light searing into your eyes—but you indulged in the sleepy softness of the high, ignored it as dreamsand, and stretched. The future was not far away. The past was getting closer.

It was getting much closer.

And then you were lying on the sofa, all comfortable heaven, Alice on top of you, and the lights were out.

To FORGIVE *Berlin for drugging you, turn to page* 202

*To accept the Supercoke, turn to page* 208

*To drift away, turn to page* 95

## 89

---

"So, do you really get it, or were you just trying to appease me?" You passed through the front door of the club and out into the cool autumn evening. "About closing the loop?"

After the crowded club, the night air grounded you, crisp and clean. "Kind of."

"Listen, can you remember any of this afternoon?"

"I can remember the *other* afternoon," you said, more as a reflex than anything. It wasn't precisely real, but it was something. What you could see was more the shadow of its memory: the camper van, a man at the door. The certainty that that wasn't what had happened.

"You can? How much?"

"Nothing. Just that it's there."

"Yeah, I get that. But we can't just have nothing there. We jumped forward, now we gotta fill it in."

"Berlin, I think that'll just—"

"I've been further out, okay? And we need to go back.

Trust me, if we just do this right, it'll all go away. I promise. Please."

You blinked. Berlin rarely said 'please,' let alone 'I promise.'

"I'm here, aren't I?"

Berlin looked like he could kiss you. "Just keep a cool head, okay? That's the most important thing."

"A cool head about what?"

"Anything. All of it. This Bob guy, we've got to deal with him."

"'Deal' with?"

"Listen, I don't know. But let's nip this thing in the bud before it gets out of control, okay?"

"That's what I was trying to do."

"I'm telling ya, this evening is a band-aid over a goddamn gouge. This guy won't stop just because we're hiding out in this little pocket. Fuck, I'm shocked it's not raining yet."

As if on cue, thunder rumbled in the distance.

"Perfect," said Berlin, "fucking perfect. That definitely didn't happen last time."

"Lin... how long have you been tripping?"

"You don't want to know. Just trust me, okay?"

*Turn to page 210*

## 90

---

"Supercoke sounds amazing," you said. "Just try not to spike this one."

"Hey. Berlin took advantage of my trust in him." She opened the fridge and withdrew a bottle.

You twisted off the seal with a fizz. "Why do you trust him? He's a drug dealer." You took your first sip. Cool and *ahhh*.

Trinity raised an eyebrow. "You live with him and you don't trust him?"

"Maybe that's the only way *to* live with him."

That one made her smirk. "Hm. Maybe so."

You lapsed into a moment of silence.

"This is helping."

"The Supercoke? Or me?" Trinity sank down into the kitchen chair across from you. There were wilting flowers in a vase on the table.

"Both," you said, "but mostly you."

"So are you going to tell me more about this time trip? Or do I just have to be slowly consumed by curiosity?"

"I don't know what I *can* tell you. It's messing with my memory. I don't even know what to say."

"How about, 'hey Trinity, want to try some?'"

"You don't want to try this."

"I think I can make my illicit drug choices for myself."

"I don't even have any," you said, but as soon as you said it you knew it wasn't true. That small square of tabs burnt white hot in your pocket. When did that happen?

"The look on your face says you totally have some."

"Shut up."

"I'm not gonna push it! I wanna help you, first and foremost. But you ought to consider it. Since I've been so helpful, after all."

You rolled your eyes at her. "Okay, maybe."

"That's all I ask."

You wanted to tell her what you knew. You wanted to take her hands in yours and, through touch telepathy, show her what had happened and how you remembered it. As it was, it was not something you could voice or put words to.

The past—or, perhaps, alternate pasts and futures—pulled on you. The force of their combined weight was slowly overcoming the pull of this present. It had started to rain, smooth and rhythmic against the kitchen window. But you took another sip of Supercoke and stayed, clinging. Out of all the realities, this was the only place you wanted to be.

TURN *to page* 2 1 1

## 91

---

"Of course," you said, straightening your back. The wind lifted your hair. "Berlin, we're gonna get out of this."

"Then we have to sink up," Berlin said. "We have to undo it."

"Undo undoing it, you mean?"

"Whatever. Face it. You know what I mean."

You did. In fact, you were already poised on the edge of the moment: back in the camper van with Berlin showing you the acid tabs.

*Turn to page 22 to remember*

## 92

---

## THE END

Trinity looked at you, expectant. You had fought for this future, you knew. Even if it meant putting on blinders and ignoring it all. Perhaps Berlin was right: you could not stay hidden forever. You could not put a bandage on a gaping wound and call it quits.

But perhaps you could for now. Perhaps "for now" was enough.

Perhaps you could stay up all night, sipping Super-coke, telling Trinity what you knew. It couldn't hurt.

Could it?

---

This is the conclusion of the ECHO6 timeline of volume 1.

TURN to page 1 to begin again

## 93

## FREE AGENT

You reached into your pocket and pulled out the sheet of acid tabs Berlin had given you. You held it out to Bob.

"Here," you said. "This is all I have."

Bob tilted his head to one side and stepped forward. He took the sheet from you, delicate, and tucked it into the breast pocket of his suit.

"Well then," Bob said. "You're just useless, aren't you?"

You prickled. You had, after all, just handed over your last resort, your only link to independence, alternate realities, and the past.

"I mean that in the kindest way possible," said Bob. "I'm always flattered when an innocent counterculture kid like yourself puts their faith in little old me. But I'm afraid you've rather told on yourself, you see. Obviously Berlin feels he can't trust you with his wares."

"He can trust me," you protested.

"He *trusted* you, perhaps," Bob said, "but as you'll soon learn, such matters are in a constant state of flux. And when you bring a factor such as tango hotel into the mix—" Bob tapped his breast pocket—"you'll find friends are much more fickle than they first seem. Come." Bob brushed by you and made his way out of the van.

You followed. "Where are we going?"

"There's no use staying here and waiting around if he's already made a break for it," Bob continued, exiting the RV and into the sparsely populated trailer park. In the distance, near the entrance, a black car was parked just beyond the gate. He headed towards it. "We'll head back to Central and head him off down the line. In the meantime, we'll get you processed."

"Processed?"

"Well, assessed, but I'll put in a good word for you. You think we're going to let you witness something like this and just walk away?"

"'We?'"

"Central. But I'm getting ahead of myself."

You had reached the car. Its license plate was black, branded with the name "BOBSMITH" in white letters. Bob opened the passenger door for you and gestured for you to climb inside.

Something in you hesitated. If only your mother could see you now. If only *Berlin* could see you now. But you had headed so far down this new hall that you couldn't turn back; even the feeble light from the crack in the distance had gone. You had made a commitment to this place, this person you were daring to be, who played by the rules of men in suits and sunglasses. You got in the car.

Bob climbed into the driver's seat and started the ignition. "Welcome," he said, "to the rest of your life."

———

This is the conclusion of the ECHO7 timeline of volume 1.

Thank you for reading volume one of *Tempus Fugit*. This story has lived in my heart for years and it is a delight to share it with you. If you enjoyed the experience, it would make a huge difference if you left a review on Amazon or Goodreads. Indie authors are the underdog in the modern marketplace and even a brief vote of confidence goes a long way.

Thank you again for your time and attention.

Best wishes, x
-Jules

———

The adventure continues in Volume 2: *Sinking Up*. Join our mailing list to be notified of its release.

# ABOUT THE AUTHOR

Jaded millenial and ex-vagrant Jules Pelarski was diagnosed with bipolar disorder in 2017 after four involuntary hospitalizations. Pelarski is an emerging science fiction writer whose short fiction was shortlisted for the Kurt Vonnegut Prize.

For information about future releases, games, and more, visit www.playtempusfugit.com

## ABOUT THE ILLUSTRATIONS

Jules Pelarski created these illustrations and the cover art using the Midjourney AI tool with reference to 1980s comic art. Midjourney is a GAN-based, CLIP-guided diffusion model that responds to human input. The version was v4.

Printed in Great Britain
by Amazon

21993909R00131